## "What happened?"

"It was a prank phone call," Tessa said hurriedly. "I got spooked."

"What did the caller say?" Henry asked.

"Nothing that made any sense."

"Can you be a little more specific?"

"He said he knew what I had done," she replied.

"There's someone you were thinking of? Someone who might want to scare you?"

"The kidnapper pops to mind," Kayla offered before Tessa could respond.

Too bad. Henry would have liked to hear Tessa's answer.

He had a feeling the kidnapper hadn't been the first person to pop into her mind. She'd told him very little about her past. But that seemed to be Tessa's MO: very little information and very few details.

He wanted to protect her.

She wasn't making it easy.

He was about to tell her that when something crashed through the window a few feet away, smashing the pane of glass and shattering it into millions of tiny shards.

"Get down!" he shouted, diving toward Tessa and tackling her to the ground as light flashed and a ball of fire shot across the room.

Aside from her faith and her family, there's not much **Shirlee McCoy** enjoys more than a good book! When she's not hanging out with the people she loves most, she can be found plotting her next Love Inspired Suspense story or trekking through the wilderness, training with a local Search and Rescue team. Shirlee loves to hear from readers. If you have time, drop her a line at shirlee@shirleemccoy.com.

### Books by Shirlee McCoy

### Love Inspired Suspense

#### FBI: Special Crimes Unit

*Night Stalker*
*Gone*
*Dangerous Sanctuary*
*Lone Witness*

#### Mission: Rescue

*Protective Instincts*
*Her Christmas Guardian*
*Exit Strategy*
*Deadly Christmas Secrets*
*Mystery Child*
*The Christmas Target*
*Mistaken Identity*
*Christmas on the Run*

#### Military K-9 Unit

*Valiant Defender*

#### Classified K-9 Unit

*Bodyguard*

Visit the Author Profile page at Harlequin.com for more titles.

# LONE WITNESS

## SHIRLEE McCOY

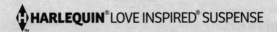
HARLEQUIN® LOVE INSPIRED® SUSPENSE

Recycling programs
for this product may
not exist in your area.

LOVE INSPIRED BOOKS

ISBN-13: 978-1-335-67900-0

Lone Witness

www.Harlequin.com

Printed in U.S.A.

Have not I commanded thee? Be strong and of a good courage; be not afraid, neither be thou dismayed: for the Lord thy God is with thee whithersoever thou goest.
–*Joshua* 1:9

To my children. Who know me well and love me anyway.

# ONE

Wind buffeted the windows of Tessa Carlson's tiny cottage, rattling the glass as she rinsed her coffee mug and set it in the sink. Outside, thick shrubs brushed against the siding, scraping against the old wood shingles, the sound eerie and unnerving. Usually, she didn't feel unsettled by the solitude of winter in Provincetown, Massachusetts. This morning, she felt a little anxious and a little off, as if all the hard work she'd done healing from the past had been wasted.

Three years, four months, twelve hours.

That's how long it had been since she'd disappeared from Napa Valley. There'd been no missing person report. No emotional plea for her return. She doubted Patrick had cared that she was gone. Although, he'd cared a lot about his reputation. To have his girlfriend walk away had to have been a blow to his ego.

Or, maybe not.

He'd moved on quickly after she'd gone, stepping into a new relationship within months of Tessa's exit from his life.

She knew, because she'd kept tabs on him. She had been afraid not to.

The man who had once been her Prince Charming, her path out of abject poverty, had become her worst nightmare. The abuse had been subtle at first. A quick insult. A veiled threat. Eventually, veiled threats had become overt. Words had become shoves and slaps. She had spent eight years believing things would get better and another planning her escape. She had known leaving was the only way to survive, but it had still been the most difficult thing she'd ever done.

She'd grown up tough. She'd had no idea who her father was, and very little idea of what a mother should be. Hers had always been hopped up on drugs or coming down from a high. There'd been nothing stable about the life she'd lived in the Los Angeles projects, but she'd been working to get herself out when she'd met Patrick.

He'd been the antithesis of everything she had hated about her life. Polished and refined, well-mannered and quick to offer compliments, he'd taken advantage of an eighteen-year-old's desperation. She could see that now. At nearly thirty, she understood that she had been groomed to be his plaything, his prize. He had never loved her. He had loved the control he had over her.

Still, nine years was a long time to be with someone. It was a long time to love someone who didn't love you.

*If* that's what her feelings for Patrick had been.

Even now, three years of contemplation later, she wasn't sure. She had thought that she'd loved him. She knew that. By the time she'd left, all she had been able to feel was terror. She had planned to run as far as she could and create a new life that he would never be able to take from her. She had done that.

If he found her, he'd be bent on destroying what she had built for herself. Out of spite. Out of a need for revenge.

And, she had unwittingly given him the perfect means to do it, because she'd grabbed everything from the wall safe in his walk-in closet the day she'd left rather than just the items that had belonged to her.

Money. Antique jewelry meant for his Napa Valley antiques store. The valuables were a drop of rain in the ocean of his wealth, but Patrick never forgot an insult. He never forgave a perceived wrong.

She shuddered, stepping away from the sink and the darkness beyond the window.

"He's married now," she reminded herself as she grabbed her coat and slid into it.

She wanted to find comfort in that, but she couldn't. Patrick had become engaged to the widow of his business partner, Ryan Wilder, less than a year after Tessa had left. Ryan had been murdered several months before Tessa fled. She had attended his funeral with Patrick and seen how deeply his widow, Sheila, had grieved. The fact that she and Patrick had married a few months ago surprised Tessa every time she thought about it.

She tried not to think about it.

Just like she tried not to think about Patrick. Skimming online articles from Napa Valley gave her quick glimpses into the high-society life she had once lived and reassured her that Patrick was busy living a life that didn't include her. She didn't miss him or the life she'd had with him. She wasn't mourning what she'd lost. She certainly wasn't jealous of Patrick's marriage.

She was worried.

Always. Every day. She lived with the fear that Patrick would find her and use the theft of his belongings as a bargaining tool to force her back into a life she hated.

If she'd been thinking clearly at the time, she would have realized taking anything out of the safe would be a mistake. Even the beautiful and expensive jewelry Patrick had gifted her during their relationship should have been left behind.

She'd been desperate to secure her future, and she had been in a rush to grab all the pricey pieces he'd given her. She'd been terrified Patrick would return home, so she hadn't taken time to look at each item. She'd taken everything and tossed it into an oversize purse before closing the safe and fleeing.

Her reason didn't make her feel better.

What she'd done was wrong.

She knew that now.

Then, all she'd known was how afraid she was.

She glanced at her watch and frowned.

Time was ticking away while she worried about a past that she had left far behind. She had a diner to open, and if she was late doing it, her boss would not be happy. Ernie wouldn't fire her, but he'd be disappointed, and he'd let her know it. He'd taken a chance when he'd promoted her to day-shift manager, and she'd worked hard to ensure that he didn't regret it.

She grabbed her purse from a hook near the door and stepped outside, locking the door and checking it twice. Just like she always did.

Even with the wind whispering through dry grass and dead leaves, the morning seemed quiet. The distant sound of waves lapping against the shore was the only reminder that Provincetown was a thriving tourist destination. In the spring and summer, the beaches teemed with people, but in the winter, the sandy windswept dunes were nearly devoid of life. That was when Tessa loved it most.

She hurried down the path that led to the road, scanning the area for signs that she wasn't alone. She didn't expect to see anyone. In the years that she'd been walking to Ernie's Diner, she'd only ever run into people during the summer months, when the sun rose early and excited vacationers rose with it. During the coldest months, she enjoyed her solitude, making the walk through the icy darkness as the sun made its way above the horizon.

The dead-end street she lived on was lined with rental cottages, all of them empty in the fall and winter. The one she occupied belonged to Ernie and his wife, Betty. They'd offered it for a good price, and she had been happy to accept.

She had been renting the place for nearly as long as she had been in the Cape Cod town. Some days it felt like home. Other days, it felt like a place to stay for a while. She'd have her nursing degree at the end of the school year. She'd take her RN exam in the summer. If she passed—

*when* she passed—she'd have good job prospects and options for where she wanted to live.

Life was working out the way she'd planned.

Maybe that was why she'd felt so anxious lately. She didn't expect good things to happen. Even when she was living right, doing right and following the rules, she expected the gavel to fall and her life to be thrown into chaos again.

Betty often told her that God had good things in store, and Tessa wanted to believe it. She certainly believed that He'd brought her to Provincetown and given her the chance she needed to begin again.

As for the rest, she wasn't sure.

She only knew she had to keep moving forward and hoping for the best.

She turned left at the end of the road, bypassing several empty houses as she walked toward the more populated residential area. Ernie's Diner was in the heart of Provincetown's business district. Sandwiched between an art gallery and a small motel, it came alive in the late spring and summer and quieted down as cold weather moved in. A skeleton crew worked through winter, and it was the manager's job to prep for the morning rush. Tessa didn't mind. She enjoyed being alone in the diner, setting the tables and sweeping the floor, checking the restrooms and the previous evening's receipts.

Even in the winter, the diner had a busy breakfast and dinner rush. She enjoyed that, too. There was something cathartic about the routine of small-town life. As much as she thought it might be best to go to a big city once she'd attained her nursing license, she couldn't help thinking about how much she'd miss Provincetown.

She sighed, the cold wind stinging her cheeks and seeping through her black slacks. She shoved her hands into her pockets, her purse thumping her as she half jogged down a narrow side street.

She could see the Pilgrim's Monument glowing in the distance, the tower standing tall against the dark morning sky. This area of town was well-lit, lights gleaming from front porches and shining down from streetlights that dotted the road. Just a few more blocks, and she'd turn onto Commercial Street. Ernie's Diner was ten blocks down. A mile and a half walk from her place but an easy one.

Even in this busier area of town, she wasn't expecting to see anyone outside before dawn. Not in the winter with the wind chill hovering just above freezing. Most people who commuted to Boston for work were already at the small regional airport, waiting to board the commuter flight. Those that worked in town were still in bed. The shadow that emerged from between two houses was so startling, she jumped back, putting an old elm between herself and the dark figure. Broad-shouldered and moving quickly, it appeared to be a man. That was enough to make her step back again. She was three houses away, frozen in fear, watching as he stepped into the street, a pile of blankets in his arms.

No. Not blankets. A child with long dark hair. One arm flopping out from beneath the covers. She told herself they were father and daughter, off on a long-weekend adventure together. But something about the child's stillness bothered her. She wasn't a mother. She had no real experience with kids, but she'd seen plenty of them in the diner—fidgeting, moving, talking…always busy. Even asleep, children seemed to be in a perpetual state of awareness. One little nudge, and they were awake and on the move.

This little girl was still, only one arm swaying with the man's loping movements. He was heading across the road—a streetlight was shining on his baseball cap, and Tessa could make out pale skin and sunglasses.

And that wasn't right, either. The sunglasses. Not before dawn.

Tessa told herself that it wasn't her business. She reminded herself that she had a lot to lose if she called attention to herself or caused any trouble in the quiet neighborhood. She tried to turn her back and pretend she hadn't seen anything, but she couldn't live with the consequences of inaction. If the next biggest news story was about a little girl stolen from her home, then what? Would Tessa step forward and give an account of what she'd seen? Too late to stop it? Too late to help?

"Good morning," she called, stepping out from behind the tree, her heart hammering against her ribs.

A tiny hesitation in his stride was the only evidence the man gave that he'd heard her.

"It's awfully cold this morning, isn't it?" she asked, following him up the street toward a Jeep that sat near the corner of the road.

"Too cold for a conversation," the man finally replied, nearly jogging now.

"Is that your daughter?"

"Mind your business, lady," he growled, the Jeep just a few yards away.

"So, she's not."

He whirled around, the cap flying from his head. He had dark hair and those sunglasses. "I said, mind your business."

The venom in his voice made the hair on her arms stand on end. She knew the tone. She knew the threat it implied. "It *is* my business, if she's not your daughter."

"She's my daughter," he growled, swinging back around and striding away.

She pulled her cell phone from her pocket and dialed 911, because she didn't dare take a chance that he was lying.

Maybe he sensed what she was doing.

Maybe he just glanced back to make certain she was no longer following. One way or another, he looked back and saw her with the phone pressed to her ear.

"Hang up," he said coldly.

"Put the girl down," she countered, the operator's voice ringing in her ear.

The man lunged, the child held in one arm, his free arm grabbing for the phone. He slapped it from Tessa's hand, then shoved her so hard she fell backward. She scrambled after the phone, desperate to give her location. He kicked it across the pavement, then sprinted to the Jeep.

Tessa screamed for help as she followed. He reached the Jeep seconds ahead of her, yanking open the back door and tossing the girl inside. He would have slammed the door closed, but Tessa grabbed his arm and pulled him away as she tried to get to the child.

She was tugging the little girl out of the Jeep when his arm snaked around her throat. She tried to scream again, but his grip was too tight and no sound would come. She had no choice but to release the girl, to claw at his arm and shove backward into his thin frame. They tumbled to the ground, his curses ringing in her ears.

She saw the barrel of the gun seconds before it was jabbed into her temple. "Get up," he ordered.

She did as she was told. Not because she was afraid to die, but because she was afraid of what would happen to the girl if he drove off alone with her.

"Get in the Jeep," he demanded.

She hesitated, desperate to find a way out of the situation. One that would save her and the little girl.

"I said, get in," he nearly screamed, slamming the barrel of the gun into the side of her head.

She saw stars, tasted blood, felt herself falling.

She knew he'd lifted her, was shoving her into the Jeep. She thought she heard someone shouting for them to stop, thought she heard the faint sound of sirens. Then the door slammed shut, and she heard nothing but the rev of the Jeep's engine as the man sped away.

Special Agent Henry Miller sprinted across the road, his focus on the Jeep that was speeding toward the intersection at the end of the street. His five-year-old daughter Everly was inside the vehicle. He was certain of that. He'd heard a woman screaming for help as he was heading down his in-laws' hall to check on his daughters. The screams had been faint but audible through the nineteenth-century windows.

He'd run to the girls' room and found the window open, frigid air wafting in. Aria had been sleeping, huddled beneath her blankets. Everly was gone.

He'd been in the house when she'd been taken.

He hadn't heard anything earlier. Just the settling of old boards and joists as he carried his overnight bag into the guest room and unpacked for the weekend. His in-laws had been in bed when he'd arrived, the girls tucked in and sleeping. The quiet was comforting, and the house had seemed as much like home as any ever had. Like every other parent who had ever woken to find a child missing, he had had no clue that anything was amiss.

Until he'd heard the scream.

"Everly!" he shouted, his heart thundering, his brain screaming that this had to be a nightmare.

There was no way his daughter could have been taken from her room, carried out a window that had been jimmied open and tossed into a Jeep that was quickly driving away.

But he'd seen the window, the cut screen, the jimmied lock.

He spun on his heels, sprinting back to his in-laws' house and the car he'd parked in the driveway less than an hour ago. The keys were in the pocket of his jacket, and that was still in the house. He reached the porch at a dead run, then glanced over his shoulder to see which direction the Jeep turned at the end of the road. Left toward Commercial Street. From there, it would be an easy drive out of town.

The front door flew open, and his mother-in-law, Rachelle, stepped outside, her face stark white. "Where's Everly?" she cried.

"I need my jacket," he responded, the words as hard and crisp as the winter air.

"Right here." His father-in-law, Brett, shoved past Rachelle, thrusting the jacket into his hands.

"Call nine-one-one. Report a kidnapping. The vehicle is a black Jeep. Newer model. Four-door. Heading toward Commercial Street."

He ran to his car and sped out of the driveway, the tires kicking up gravel as he turned onto the paved road. A purse sat near the curb, a phone several yards away from it. He'd seen a woman and man struggling with one another as he'd rounded the side of the house. She'd been shoved into the Jeep. Everly wasn't alone. That didn't make the situation any better.

He'd already lost his wife, Diane, in gun-fire from a drive-by shooting. She'd been eight months pregnant with Everly and her twin sister, Aria. The surgeon had been able to save the girls, but Diane's injury had proven fatal.

The heartache of saying goodbye to his wife had brought him to his knees. He didn't think he could survive losing one of his daughters, too.

He rounded the corner at the end of the street, taking the turn so fast, he wasn't sure all the tires stayed on the ground. Commercial Street was quiet as the shops that were usually bustling with life were dormant and dark, though a few exterior lights illuminated doorways and outdoor eating areas. Diane had loved Provincetown. It had been her family's summer home when she was growing up. Now that she was gone, her parents lived there nearly year-round. Henry and the girls visited often, and they always spent the weekend closest to Diane's birthday in town.

This was that weekend.

He'd had a full docket at work, and he hadn't been able to take Friday off. His in-laws had picked the girls up after school and made the three-hour drive. He had finally clocked out of work just before midnight. He'd almost spent the night in Boston. He'd been that tired, that ready for sleep. But the girls had been looking forward to their yearly breakfast on the winter-cold beach—blankets spread on the sand, the sun rising above the ocean. All of them bundled up and pink-cheeked, adults sipping coffee. Kids drinking cocoa.

He hadn't wanted to disappoint them, so he'd made the long drive, stopping a few times to drink black coffee and wake himself up. What if he'd stayed in Boston? Would he have arrived in the morning and been the first to realize Everly was missing?

He shuddered, forcing away that thought, and the fear. He needed to stay focused on the task. Taillights gleamed in the distance, as the car ahead cruised through the business district at a pace that was probably just under the speed limit. The driver had no intention of being pulled over for speeding. If he made it to Route 6, it would be easy for him to find a place to pull off the road and hide. There were small towns dotting the Cape, and plenty of places for someone to disappear if he wanted to. Henry couldn't let him. For Everly's sake, and for the sake of the woman who'd been thrown in the Jeep with her, he had to stop the driver before he made it out of Provincetown.

He accelerated to a dangerous speed, whizzing past shops as he closed in on the fleeing vehicle. The driver must have realized he was being followed. He took a hard turn onto a side street, the back wheel bouncing over the sidewalk. Henry did the same, easing up on the accelerator as he rounded the turn.

The Jeep had slowed, as the driver navigated the narrow side street and headed south. Henry's cell buzzed. He ignored it. The Jeep slowed more, turning into an alley that Henry had walked down dozens of times when he and Diane were dating.

His hands tightened on the steering wheel, his heart galloping, the pace fast and erratic. He'd held Diane's hand at the hospital after the shooting and promised her that everything would be all right, and that no matter what, he'd take care of their daughters. When the surgeon had told him Diane was brain-dead, he'd sat by her side and told her how much she'd meant to him, how fortunate and blessed he'd been to have her in his life.

And he'd promised her that the girls would be fine.

That he'd make certain they had wonderful lives.

He'd promised that they would know who she was and how much they'd meant to her.

He'd spent nearly six years working to fulfill those promises. He refused to fail now. He refused to believe that Everly would be taken from him, that she'd disappear like so many other children had. That he'd spend the rest of his life searching the faces of strangers, hoping to see his daughter.

The Jeep cleared the alley and bounced onto Conwell Street. Henry followed, the traffic light at Route 6 glowing green. It turned red as the Jeep approached. The driver slowed and then stopped. Perhaps out of caution. Perhaps out of habit.

Henry was closing the distance between them, not trying to hide the fact that he was following. He'd let the guy know he'd been seen, that what he'd tried to do under the cover of darkness had been exposed.

The light turned green as Henry neared the back bumper of the Jeep. He thought about clipping it, but worried that Everly would be hurt.

As the Jeep turned onto the highway, the back door flew open and a woman jumped out, Everly clutched against her chest. She stumbled and fell, skidding across the pavement on her knees, her arms still tight around his daughter.

She was up in a flash, sprinting toward buildings that she probably hoped would offer her cover or a place to hide. Everly hadn't moved. She was limp as a rag doll, bouncing against the woman's shoulder.

Henry threw the SUV into Park and jumped out, racing after her. Not caring about protocol, about securing the perpetrator, about doing any of the things he'd been trained to do. He was only worried about how still Everly was. How quiet. How completely unlike the bubbly little girl he knew her to be.

"FBI! Slow down and let me help you," he called as he sprinted after the woman.

She didn't believe him, of course.

She'd been traumatized and was running for her life with a child in her arms. He doubted his words had even registered. He'd spoken to victims of violent crimes. He'd interviewed witnesses. He knew how difficult it was to process information when the brain was bent on survival.

He tried again. "Ma'am! Stop! Let me help you!"

She darted between two buildings and entered an alley much too narrow for a vehicle.

He was right behind her, catching up fast. His attention was on Everly's arm, flopping against the woman's back. He'd never seen his daughter unresponsive. She was always filled with energy and verve. Unlike her twin, she was outgoing and talkative, her mouth running as often and as fast as her nearly six-year-old feet.

"Everly!" he called as he finally caught up to the woman. He grabbed her narrow shoulder, yanking her backward.

She whirled toward him, her arms wrapped around his daughter, her eyes wide with fear.

"Back off," she panted.

"I'm her father," he responded, dragging her farther away from the opening of the alley.

"You said you were with the FBI," she replied, trying to pull away.

"I am."

"You can't have it both ways. You can't be her father and with the FBI."

"Why not?"

She scowled. "I already called the police. I can hear the sirens. They'll be here any minute."

He could hear the sirens, too, wailing in the distance, shouting that help was on the way.

Only help had no way of knowing where they were, and the perp was still on the loose. "Come on. Let's get away from the street."

He pulled her toward the far end of the alley, past a Dumpster and pile of dismantled cardboard boxes.

Something scuffled on the cement behind them.

He glanced at the entrance to the alley as a dark figure stepped into view. Tall and lean, his face hidden by the shadows, he took a step forward and pulled something from beneath his jacket.

Henry jerked the woman sideways, shoving

her behind the Dumpster. He followed, throwing himself in front of her and Everly as the first bullet shattered the quiet and slammed into the metal near his head.

# TWO

A bullet pinged off the brick building, the casing dropping to the ground and rolling under trash that littered the alley. Another slammed into the ground just beyond the Dumpster they were hiding behind.

Sirens screamed in the distance, but help was too far away. The next bullet could pierce the metal and slam into Tessa, the little girl she carried or the man who'd shoved them behind the Dumpster.

"We need to get out of here!" Tessa yelled as a third bullet hit the building just above them. Bits of brick and mortar rained down, clattering onto the ground and skipping across the concrete.

"It's okay," the man said, pressing her into the old brick wall. She knew the alley, the buildings on either side—a barber shop and an art shop— the streets that crossed in front and behind it. She knew where she was, but she doubted the police did, and she doubted that staying where they were was going to make anything okay.

"It is not okay," she whispered, shoving against his solid weight, the little girl still in her arms.

"It will be," he replied.

"How do you know?"

"He's not going to come around the Dumpster. He has no idea if I'm armed."

"*He* is armed. That's what's going to matter to him."

"What is going to matter to him is escaping. He might want to get rid of a witness, but he won't risk losing his freedom to do it."

It made sense, but that didn't make her feel any less like a sitting duck.

She shivered, her body smashed between the wall and the man.

She hated the feeling of helplessness that brought, the memories that clawed at the back of her mind. Other dark mornings and late nights when fear had made her cower and beg. When she'd fled Patrick, she'd promised herself that she would never do those things again. That she would fight or go down trying to.

She tried to move, but the man was a solid mass of muscle and sinew, all of it focused on keeping her where she was.

"Let me go," she demanded, her voice shaking.

She hated that as much as she hated feeling helpless.

He stepped back, just enough to let her breathe. She inhaled cold air and baby shampoo. She'd done what she'd set out to do. She'd kept a child from being kidnapped. Now, she wanted to go to the diner and get back to the familiar routine of prepping for opening. That felt safe to her, and it felt more right than staying in the cold alley waiting for the police to arrive.

"I need to get to my job," she murmured.

"Your boss will understand if you don't show up," the man said gently, reaching for the little girl and taking her from Tessa's arms.

"You don't know my boss."

"No. I don't," he said, his attention on the child.

"He's counting on me to open the diner."

"The police will want to speak to you first."

"They can find me at Ernie's." She knew it was unreasonable. She knew that she needed to stay where she was. The police would want to speak to her. She'd have to give a statement. There'd be dozens of questions about what had happened and what she'd seen.

But, all she wanted to do was walk away.

Just like she'd done three years ago.

She knew that wouldn't solve anything. Running from problems never did. Her grandmother used to tell her that. The one person in her childhood who had actually cared, Hester had done her best to give Tessa a firm foundation on which she could build a better future.

It had taken way too many years for Tessa to do that.

"The police will know where that is," she continued.

"You're in shock. You're not thinking clearly. If you were, you'd realize that the best thing for you and my daughter is to wait here until police and medics arrive," the man said in the calm and patient tone she would have used with a screaming toddler tossing biscuits on the floor of the diner.

"Is she really your daughter?" she asked.

"Yes."

"I'm sorry this happened to her."

"Me, too," he responded, frowning as he looked at the little girl. "She's never this soundly asleep. Everly?" He brushed a strand of hair from her cheek.

"Her pulse is good. I checked in the Jeep."

"Thank you for doing that, and for saving her." He shrugged out of his jacket and spread it on the ground, stepping far enough away that Tessa could have left if she'd really wanted to. He laid Everly on the coat, checking her pulse and then running his hands down her arms and legs.

"No breaks," he murmured, reaching into his back pocket and tossing a phone in Tessa's direction. "Can you call nine-one-one? Give the police our location and ask for an ambulance. Make sure they know this is related to the report of a kidnapping."

She made the call, her hands shaking, her voice trembling. When the operator asked for her name, she hesitated before giving it. She'd worked hard to create a life she could be proud of, one she thought that God would approve of and that her grandmother, who'd died when she was fourteen, would have applauded. She was risking that by allowing herself to be drawn into someone else's drama. The fact was, in the past, she'd done things she wasn't proud of. None of the people in her new life knew that. None of them really knew her. Not the real her. She wanted to keep it that way.

But, she also wanted to help.

She wanted to make certain that the person who'd tried to kidnap Everly didn't try to kidnap another child. She wanted to do the right thing, because it was right. Even if it cost her everything she'd worked for.

She crouched next to the man and his daughter, watching as he checked the little girl's bruised shins and bare feet. He pushed up the sleeves of her nightgown, turned her arms so the exterior building lights fell on them. There was a smudge of blood on one arm, and he paused, studying it for a moment.

"What is it?" she asked.

"Puncture wound. She was drugged." He took off his flannel shirt and tucked it around Everly, his face hard, his expression unreadable. He had a five-o'clock shadow on his chin and dark circles beneath his eyes. Short hair. Muscular build. Even if he hadn't told her he was with the FBI, she'd have guessed he was law enforcement or military.

"Your wife must be worried sick," she said, imagining the girl's mother waiting at home, praying that her daughter would be returned. "Maybe you should call her and let her know you found Everly?"

She handed him the phone, and he tucked it into his pocket. "Her mother died the day she and her twin were born."

"I'm sorry for your loss," she said.

"Thank you. It was difficult. Some days, it still is. Diane was a wonderful person. She would have been a great mother. I wish she would have at least had the chance to meet her daughters."

"I can't imagine how hard it must have been

to grieve her loss while trying to take care of two newborns."

"They were in the NICU for a while, and my in-laws were a huge help. By the time I brought the girls home, I had people lined up to step in and help out. I'm very fortunate in my friends, and I'm very fortunate tonight ended as well as it did." He touched Everly's cheek, tucked the shirt around her a little more tightly.

Police lights flashed on the pavement and a radio crackled. Help had arrived. Soon half the population of Provincetown would be aware of the attempted kidnapping. People would be congregating on the street, trying to get a look at the girl and her rescuers. There would be local reporters jockeying for position, trying to get the best photo and the best answers to the most insightful questions.

A story like this could make national news.

And Tessa couldn't afford to be part of that.

She stepped away from the Dumpster, and the man, easing toward the back of the alley. It led to a side street that would take her to Ernie's Diner if she followed it long enough. She'd already given her name to the 911 operator. The kidnapper was probably halfway to the mainland by now. If he was smart, he'd never return.

She'd go to work. She'd open the diner. She'd

go on with her day and hope that her name would be overlooked or misplaced or forgotten.

It was a vain hope, of course.

They recorded 911 calls.

Eventually, the police would track her down and interview her. She'd be happy to provide whatever information she could. Right now, though, she was going to put distance between herself and the drama. She took another few steps away, shivering as cold wind whipped through the narrow alley and scattered bits of debris. The sun had begun its ascent, and the sky was gray with deferred light. She could see Everly clearly—the soft slope of her chin and cheek, the darkness of her lashes. Her father had pulled the edges of his coat around her tiny body, and his dark T-shirt clung to broad shoulders and a firm abdomen. He had to be cold, but he didn't shiver. His focus was on his daughter, and that gave Tessa plenty of opportunity to leave.

*God, please don't let anything horrible be wrong with Everly*, Tessa prayed silently as she shuffled backward.

A police officer stepped into view, his radio crackling as he hurried toward Everly.

Tessa turned and walked away.

She knew how it was done. She'd done it before, parking the Cadillac Escalade that Patrick had given her for her birthday in a mall parking lot and walking away as if she had every intention of returning. Head high, like she'd been doing nothing wrong, the backpack slung over her shoulder filled with everything she'd needed to escape.

Shoulders straight, chin up and a quick stride that didn't seem rushed. She did the same now. Confident. Focused. Completely unremarkable.

The alley was short and she walked out of it without anyone trying to stop her. She turned onto a narrow through street that was really nothing more than a paved path. Maybe she wouldn't go to the diner. Maybe she'd go back to the cottage, gather what she could and leave town. She'd done it before. She could do it again. Make her escape. Start fresh.

She thought she heard someone call her name, but she didn't look back. There wasn't a police officer in Provincetown who hadn't eaten at the diner. They knew her, and they knew how to find her.

For now.

That might change, because she didn't feel safe, like she had the day she'd driven into town and seen the ocean stretching out to one side and the bay to the other. It had been summer, the streets crowded, the beaches filled, but she'd felt solitude in the ocean breeze and peace in the warm sunlight streaming from the cloudless sky.

Cold wind blew through her cotton shirt. It had been crisp white and wrinkle-free when she'd left home. Now it was crinkled and smudged with dirt. She wiped at the spot, shivering as she checked for the key she always carried in the pocket of her slacks. It was still there. She'd dropped her purse. It was probably lying on the road, her identification and bank card easy pickings for anyone who might find them. She'd lost her phone. It had probably shattered when she'd dropped it.

"That is the least of your worries," she muttered as she wound her way behind commercial properties and, finally, walked out onto Commercial Street. She could see the bay from here, silvery blue in the lightening gloom.

She glanced back, but no one was following.

The medical and emergency-response teams were busy helping Everly.

Headlights illuminated the grayish world and an SUV drove past. Provincetown was waking, and the people who made it their year-round home would soon be out and about. According to her watch, she was twenty minutes late for her shift. The diner was still dark, the garish neon sign Ernie had purchased when he'd opened the place hanging listlessly from the clapboard siding near the gabled roof. The building had been around for over a hundred years. Some people said it had been a tavern back in the days when Provincetown had been a haven for writers, actors and freethinkers. Now it was a haven for people who enjoyed quiet and anonymity, who craved peace the way others craved chocolate.

Tessa unlocked the front door and stepped into the dining area, her heart still racing, her body almost numb with cold and fear. She had prep work to do before the line cook arrived— setting the daily special, putting out silverware and making sure the closing crew had cleaned the place to Ernie's standards. This time of year, staff was cut in half, days were slower and profits were slimmer. Ernie demanded a high work ethic from his employees and expected them to do whatever jobs were necessary to keep the place going.

Tessa had proven herself to him and to his wife. Unlike her husband, Betty had a soft edge and a warm nature. As far as Tessa knew, they'd never had children.

Of course, she hadn't asked.

She'd come to Ernie's for a job. Not for friendship or support.

She flicked on the lights, hung her coat on a hook near the door and hurried across the room, grabbing the cart of napkin-wrapped silverware from its place near the waitress station and rolling it into the dining room. There was seating for one hundred there. The patio out back seated another twenty, the view of the bay making it a prime location during the tourist season.

It was so much easier to think about that than to think about the attempted kidnapping. Everly. The man with the gun and the pale face. Her breath caught as she set silverware on place settings and tried not to hear the sirens that were still screeching in the distance. This type of crime didn't happen in Provincetown. Kidnapping wasn't a thing in the quaint artsy community.

Someone knocked on the diner's glass front door and she screamed, whirling toward the sound, a set of silverware falling to the ground. She recognized Ernie immediately, his white hair gleaming in the exterior light as he unlocked the door and stepped in, Betty close behind him. A police officer followed, standing in the entryway, her hat in her hand, her gaze fixed on Tessa.

"Tessa! What in tarnation are you doing, girl! You were just involved in a kidnapping. The police scanners are going crazy!" Ernie charged toward her, his white beard making him look like an angry grizzled gnome. "And you're here, setting silverware on the tables!"

"Ernie! Hush! Can't you see she's in shock?!" Betty said, taking off her coat and wrapping Tessa in scratchy wool and day-old perfume.

"And, look." Betty touched a throbbing spot on Tessa's temple. "What a goose egg! She probably has a concussion. You probably have a concussion," she repeated, cupping Tessa's cheeks and looking into her eyes.

"I'm okay," Tessa protested.

"Of course, you're not," Betty replied. "You've been through a terrible trauma, you got knocked in the head. More than likely, you feared for your life. Right?"

"Yes," she murmured, trying to avoid looking anywhere except Betty's face. As a child, Tessa had often lain in bed, listening to her mother partying with her newest boyfriend and wondering what it would be like to have a mother who cared. In her imagination, that kind of mother had always looked like Betty—soft face, soft eyes, soft curves and easy smile.

"Exactly. You're not thinking straight. That's why you left the scene instead of sticking around to talk to the police."

It wasn't a question, but Tessa nodded.

"It seemed to the responding officer that you were fleeing the scene. I told him that probably wasn't the case. Fleeing would make no sense, seeing as how we all know exactly where to find you," the officer said, and Tessa finally met her eyes.

Holly Williams had joined the Provincetown Police Department a few months after Tessa arrived in town. Young and brash, she had a no-nonsense approach to life that was obvious when she ate at the diner and when she attended the church they both belonged to. She didn't suffer fools gladly, and she certainly wouldn't believe lies. Not that Tessa planned to tell any. She hadn't told anyone in Provincetown about her old life, but she hadn't lied about it either. She'd simply come to town with a new identity, found a job and made a home for herself. If people asked about the past, she sidestepped the questions or gave vague answers that excluded details.

"I wasn't fleeing. I was scheduled to open today, and I didn't want to let Ernie and Betty down." It wasn't an explanation. Not really.

Holly noticed.

She eyed Tessa for a moment. Then, she shrugged. "I'm certain you know better than to leave the scene of a crime, Tessa. But, it does look like you took quite a hit."

"I guess I did." She touched the sore spot, felt the swollen lump and winced.

"Head injuries do strange things to people.

How about I have an ambulance transport you to the hospital? I'll take your statement there."

"I don't need an ambulance," Tessa said, but she did feel woozy and a little sick.

She dropped into a chair, the room spinning crazily.

"Tessa, you're white as a sheet." Ernie cupped her shoulder, his voice gentler than she'd ever heard it. "And your forehead is the color of a ripe eggplant. Go get checked out. Betty and I will handle things here. Once the morning crew shows up, we'll come to the hospital. If you're ready to be released, we'll bring you home."

"I have a ten-hour shift today. I agreed to work extra because I have that test next week, remember?" That was the truth. She did have a test. One of her last of the semester. She was so close to finishing her degree, she could almost taste it.

If she left town, she'd lose the progress she had made.

If she walked away, she'd have to leave all those hard-earned credits behind. She would have to leave the diner behind, and Ernie and Betty.

"You can still take time off for the test, but you're not working today." Ernie took her arm and helped her to her feet. He'd celebrated his seventieth birthday a few months ago, but he had the strength and energy of a man in his fifties. He had been more of a father to her than any man. He'd taught her how to run the diner, how to balance the books. He'd supported her efforts to get her degree, and he'd cheered her on, in his gruff way.

"Ernie, I can't leave you in a lurch," she protested.

"What lurch? It's winter. We barely need more than ourselves to keep things going this time of year," Betty responded.

"She's right," Ernie agreed. "Can you take her to the hospital, Holly? I want to make certain she goes straight there."

"Ernie, really," Tessa protested. "I have school bills to pay, and I need to—"

"Don't say another word about it, honey," Betty said. "We've got you covered. Everything will be fine."

"I really don't need to go to the hospital." It was an hour away, and she didn't want to spend any amount of time in a police cruiser with Holly. She wasn't afraid to answer questions about the kidnapping. She was worried about saying too much about herself. Or, too little. Holly seemed like the kind of person who would pick up on the fact that Tessa never gave straight answers about where she'd come from or why she'd settled in Provincetown.

"I can take you to the police station instead," Holly interjected, her tone firm and her gaze direct. "It's up to you."

There was a threat there. Tessa heard it. Leaving the scene had been a mistake. She should have realized how big of one *before* she'd done it.

Betty was right.

She hadn't been thinking straight, but she needed to start. There would probably be a media blitz at the police station, and Tessa wanted no part of that.

"I suppose it wouldn't be a bad thing to have a doctor look at my head," she murmured, touching the sore spot.

"That's what I thought you'd say," Holly replied, taking her arm and urging outside.

Dawn had broken over the bay, bathing the town in a golden haze. The sky was deep pink, with dark clouds looming on the horizon. A winter storm was blowing in. She could feel moisture in the air, taste it in the salty wind that blew across the bay.

She hoped the weather would keep the gawkers away. She hoped it would prevent outsiders from arriving with cameras and questions.

She hoped, but she wasn't counting on it.

She had the sinking feeling that everything she had worked for had been undone, and all she could do was pray she didn't come undone with it.

She shuddered as she climbed into the front seat of Holly's cruiser and closed the door.

Henry paced the corridor outside Everly's hospital room, his cell phone in hand, his body humming with adrenaline. According to the physician who'd examined her, his daughter would be fine. She had been drugged but was otherwise unharmed. Blood tests had been taken and sent to the lab. They'd soon know what she'd been injected with.

Henry suspected they'd find midazolam in her system.

The thought filled him with dread.

In the past eighteen months, five young children had been taken from their homes. Each had been missing for several days and then been found dazed and alone at nearby public schools or medical clinics. The kidnappings had happened in small New England towns. All the victims had midazolam in their systems. All had multiple needle marks on their arms and legs. All had obvious signs of abuse but no memory of what had happened. Girls. Ranging in age from five to eight years. All of them pretty and dark-haired.

Just like Everly.

His hand clenched, his body tense with anger and frustration. The FBI special crimes unit had been working the case for several months, putting together a profile of the kidnapper and trying to find a pattern in either timing or location of the crimes.

Thus far, they had little to go on.

The perp was careful. He left no DNA evidence. No fingerprints. Nothing that would identify him. But he had an MO. One that was easily recognizable to anyone who'd read over the case files. He targeted older homes with poor security. He took children from quiet residential areas that had easy access to interstate roads. He struck in the early morning hours. Before dawn but after midnight. He cut through window screens and jimmied locks with silent precision.

Parents didn't realize what had happened until they went to wake their daughters in the morning. Hours later. When it was too late to do anything but panic and call the police.

That would have been Everly's story.

It would have been his.

If not for a stranger's timely intervention, he would have walked into his daughters' room and realized every parent's worst nightmare had come true.

He pivoted, opening Everly's door and peeking in. She was still out, tucked under layers of blankets—her dark hair had been braided by the nurse who sat by her side.

Briana or Brittany. He couldn't remember which.

A police officer stood near a curtained window, his hand resting on the butt of his firearm. He didn't speak. Just nodded in Henry's direction.

The nurse smiled. "She's still out, Mr. Miller. The doctor said it could be several hours."

"I know," he replied.

"She'll be okay. She looks good. Vitals great. Heart rate, respiration, oxygen, all of it normal. You can have my seat, if you'd like to hold her hand. Sometimes, that makes parents feel better."

He knew that.

He'd witnessed it firsthand with the parents of the girls who'd been kidnapped and returned. He'd stood in hospital rooms, asking questions as delicately as he could while they clutched the hands of the children they'd almost lost forever. Eventually, the perp might change his MO. Eventually, the girls might not be returned. He and his colleagues suspected the kidnappings were part of a child-pornography ring, and they were desperate to shut it down.

They *would* shut it down.

Not just because Everly had nearly been taken, but because every child deserved to have a safe and carefree childhood. He couldn't change all the evils in the world, but he could change some of them. For as long as he could, for as many years as he was allowed, that was what he planned to do.

"Thanks. I'll probably do that after I take the call I'm waiting on." He smiled, because he knew his voice and tone were gruff. He felt raw and ripped open, his emotions exposed in a way he wasn't used to.

"Sounds good." She returned his smile and picked up a paperback, burying her nose in it as he closed the door.

The hospital was taking every precaution.

The local police were doing the same.

Henry appreciated that. He appreciated the fact that Everly was okay. She hadn't been harmed. She'd have no memory of being kidnapped, no residual fear or trauma to recover from.

He still wished he'd been more careful. He'd known the security at his in-laws' house was lacking. He had known the windows were old. He had also known that a serial kidnapper was on the loose targeting girls his daughters' age.

But he had not thought it could happen to his family. He hadn't wanted to believe that tragedy would strike twice in one lifetime. That God would allow him to suffer again. Not the way he had when Diane died.

He hadn't prepared, and he hadn't planned. He had almost paid the price for that. He wouldn't make the same mistake again.

His phone rang, and he answered it, his voice terse. "Miller here."

"This is not your fault," his supervisor, Wren Santino, said, her tone brisk and business-like.

"When did you become a mind reader?" he replied, pacing a few feet from the room and then back again. His in-laws were on the way. He'd asked them to bring Aria. He wanted to keep both girls as close as possible until the perp was caught.

And he *would* be caught.

Henry had been able to provide a description of the Jeep. No plate number, but he was hopeful exterior security cameras at local businesses might offer more identifying features.

And then there was the witness.

Tessa Carlson. When she had disappeared from the scene, Henry had been afraid she might not be found. Fortunately, she worked at a Provincetown diner and everyone on the local police force seemed to know her. She had been easy to track down. He was hopeful she had been able to provide a description of the perpetrator.

"It doesn't take a mind reader to know what you're thinking," Wren said. "According to the message you left, Everly was possibly drugged with midazolam. I'm sure you're making the same connections I am."

"What other connections are there?"

"It's possible another drug was used. If that is the case, this may be the job of a copycat."

"Copying what? Information about the kidnappings hasn't been released to the public."

"The public may not realize a serial kidnapper is on the loose, but the stories haven't been kept quiet."

"The information about the girls being drugged has," he argued, because he knew in his gut that the man who'd attempted to take Everly was the same one who had kidnapped the other girls.

"I know, and I'm not saying you're wrong in making these connections. I'm just saying we need confirmation before we can say anything with any certainty."

"Agreed." Because, that was the way investigations were run. Gather the facts rather than make assumptions based on hunches.

"Have you had a chance to speak with the witness?" Wren asked.

"Not yet. She has a head injury and is being treated. She did leave the scene after the police arrived. They had to track her to her place of employment."

"That's interesting."

"If by interesting you mean suspicious, I agree."

"You don't think she was involved in the attempted kidnapping, do you?" Wren asked, the sudden sharpness in her voice letting him know that she was very interested in his answer.

He thought about the way Tessa had looked when she'd jumped out of the Jeep, with Everly held to her chest as she'd skidded across the pavement on her knees. She could have left his daughter behind. She had had no idea that he was following. "No, I don't. But I think she's hiding something."

"If it's not illegal, it's none of our business."

"Right now, my only business is making sure the guy who tried to kidnap my daughter is found and tossed in jail."

"I understand. The team and I are standing behind you. We'll do whatever it takes to make certain your girls stay safe and that the kidnapper is brought to justice. Jessica and I are on our way to Provincetown. We should be there in a couple of hours. See what you can get out of the witness before we arrive, okay? I'm curious to match her description with Jessica's profile of the kidnapper."

"Will do. I'll give you the information I gather when you arrive," he assured her.

"Great. See you soon, Henry." She disconnected, and he slid the phone into his pocket, his gaze shifting to the end of the hall and the elevator doors that were opening.

His in-laws stepped out, Aria between them, mittened hands clutching theirs, her cheeks pink from the cold. She was a quieter version of her sister. Introspective and introverted, she tended to allow Everly to lead the way into new adventures. She would have been lost without her sister.

"Daddy!" she cried, breaking free and running toward him.

"Hey, munchkin!" he responded, lifting her and giving her a hug that might have been just a little too tight.

"I'm not a munchkin. I'm a young lady," Aria corrected him, her expression somber and serious.

"Of course, you aren't a munchkin. That's just a figure of speech."

"I know, but I wanted to remind you. Where's Everly?" she asked. "Nana said she was at the hospital, but I didn't believe her. Sister never gets sick."

"You're right. She doesn't, but Nana never

tells tales, either. Your sister really is here." He set Aria on her feet and kissed her forehead.

"Why?" she asked, holding onto his hand and looking up into his face.

The girls were identical, their eyes the same shade of blue, their hair the same raven-black, but Aria was shorter and seemingly frailer, her scrawny frame currently hidden beneath layers of fabric and a heavy winter coat.

"She was sleeping a little too hard, and I got worried, so I brought her here," he replied, trying to give her a response that would make sense to a not-quite six-year-old.

"That's silly, Daddy," she replied. "You always sleep too hard, and we don't take you to the hospital."

"Yes, but I'm not your sister. You know she barely ever sleeps, and when she does, she's always easy to wake."

"That's true. Maybe, I should check on her. She's probably scared," she said with a frown.

"She's still asleep, but you can see her." He met his mother-in-law's eyes. "I'm sure Nana and Pop-pop won't mind bringing you in the room. I have a few things I need to take care of."

"Of course we wouldn't," Rachelle said, her voice trembling. She stepped into the hospital room, urging Aria to follow. She was as shaken as Henry and trying not to show it. A long-time

ER nurse, she usually had a calm approach to emergencies. Right now, she seemed on the edge of falling apart.

He started to follow, worried about her as much as he was about the girls.

Brett touched his shoulder. "She's okay," he said.

"She looks shaken."

"She is, but she'd rather not know that we know it." Brett ran a hand through his thick gray hair. "I feel terrible about this, Henry."

"Nothing that happened is your fault. You and Rachelle have nothing to feel bad about."

"I should have put new windows in. Better locks. A security system."

"Provincetown is a safe community. You had no way of knowing something like this would happen."

"Maybe not, but I still feel terrible. How is Everly?"

"The doctor said she would be fine."

"And the other victim? I heard she had a head injury."

It took a moment for the words to make sense.

Henry had been thinking of Tessa as a witness.

Brett was right, though. She was also a victim.

"I haven't heard much except that she's been admitted."

"I wonder if there is anything I can to do help.

We owe her a lot. If she hadn't intervened, our Everly might not be with us." A semiretired neurosurgeon, Brett had earned a reputation as being one of the best in his field. He still taught classes and gave lectures, and if it was warranted, assisted in cutting-edge neurosurgeries in Boston.

"I spoke to her before the ambulance transported Everly. She seemed lucid, but I'm going to check on her. I'll let you know if things are worse than I suspect."

"Rachelle and I will stay close to the girls until you're back," Brett said, his dark eyes so much like Diane's that Henry had to look away.

"Thanks. I'll hurry."

"Take your time. We'll work out a plan of action when you return." Brett stepped into the room and closed the door.

Henry hesitated for just long enough to convince himself that a police officer, a nurse and his in-laws were plenty of protection for the girls. Then he walked to the nurses' station and asked for Tessa's room number.

The nurse gave it after she checked a master list of people who were allowed information about and access to Tessa and Everly. It was a short list. One Henry had helped create.

Hospital staff were on high alert, watching

for unusual activity and turning away the press, who was already gathering outside the hospital.

A little girl had nearly been kidnapped.

A stranger had saved her.

There would be no hiding that from the local press, and Henry was confident national syndicates would pick up the story. For now, the hospital and police were keeping the victim's identity and the identity of the hero who'd intervened secret.

That was normal protocol, but this wasn't a normal case.

Not to Henry.

The perpetrator preyed on innocent children.

The victim was his daughter.

And he owed Tessa Carlson more than he could ever repay.

He would keep that debt in the forefront of his mind when he questioned her. He would also remember Brett's comment—Tessa was a victim, too. But he wanted answers, and he wanted them quickly. He wanted to know why she'd walked away when the police arrived. He wanted to know what she'd seen, and what she was hiding.

He wanted to take whatever information she had and use it to track down the monster who had gone after Everly and who wouldn't stop preying on the innocent until he was caught.

That was Henry's goal and his mission, and he wouldn't allow Tessa's obvious reluctance keep him from achieving it.

# THREE

Tessa's experience with law enforcement had never been good. As a child living in the projects in Los Angeles, she'd been pulled out of bed dozens of times, taken outside by stone-faced officers who were more interested in checking her room for drugs than in making certain she wasn't traumatized. She'd learned to wear street clothes to bed, so that she didn't have to face the embarrassment of being outside in her threadbare nightclothes or too-small shorts and tank top. There had been many times when she'd watched as her mother was handcuffed and carted away. She had sat in the back of police cruisers waiting for her grandmother to walk the half mile that separated their rentals, inhaling the scent of vomit and urine while she tried not to cry.

Life in the projects had not been easy.

Being her mother's daughter had not been easy.

Both had taught her the importance of staying on the right side of the law, steering clear of trouble and avoiding the police at all costs.

She tried not to show any of that as she perched on the edge of the hospital bed and answered Chief Carmichael Simpson's questions. Dressed in street clothes, his short-cropped hair sprinkled with gray, he paced her room, a pad of paper in one hand, a pen in the other. Two uniformed officers stood near the door. Darrell Mitchel and Kayla Delphina were regulars at the diner, and Kayla attended Faith Community Church. Other than that, Tessa knew nothing about her and nothing about Darrell. Right now, she wouldn't have minded a connection, a smiling face, someone aside from the taciturn police chief to focus on.

"So, what you're saying is that you were walking to work before dawn in thirty-five-degree weather when the forecasters were calling for freezing rain?" Chief Simpson said, a hint of disbelief in his voice.

At least, that was what she thought she was hearing.

It was possible her perception was tainted by past bad experiences. Patrick had questioned and criticized everything, and she'd learned to always be on guard.

She swallowed a terse reply and plastered on the smile she wore when she had to deal with frustrating customers at the diner. "My car is on its last legs, Chief Simpson. I try to put as little mileage on it as possible."

"It's about two miles from your place to the diner." He glanced at his notepad as if it contained the information. She knew it didn't. Like everyone else in town, he knew where she lived. Like everyone else, he knew she walked most days in most kinds of weather.

"That's right, and as I'm sure you know, I almost always choose to walk," she responded, the smile still plastered to her face.

"Even in the winter?" he asked.

"It's winter now, and I was walking outside," she pointed out.

"That's not an answer," he murmured.

"Walking to work is not a crime, Chief," Kayla commented, crossing her arms over her chest. "I walk around after dark all the time. Provincetown has a low crime rate."

"Point noted, officer," the chief said, his focus still on the notebook. "But I believe I directed the question at Ms. Carlson."

"As Officer Delphina pointed out, it's a safe town. I walk to work all the time. You can ask my boss, Ernie Baylor. He owns the diner," Tessa said.

"We all know who Ernie is, Ms. Carlson. We all know the diner," the chief replied, finally meeting her eyes. "If I'm giving you the impression that you've done something wrong, I apologize. You saved a little girl's life, and you deserve all the praise that's coming to you. But I don't like when these sorts of things happen in my town. The kidnapping of a child is something I take very seriously, and I want to get to the bottom of it as quickly as—"

Someone knocked on the door and it opened, a tall, sandy-haired man stepping into the room. He looked familiar, his hard face and lean muscular form reminding her of someone.

"Tessa," he said, striding toward her and offering a hand. "I'm Henry Miller. Everly's father."

Of course!

"Special Agent Miller," the chief said, before she could respond. "How is your daughter?"

"Call me Henry, and she's still unconscious, but the doctor says she will make a full recovery."

"I'm relieved to hear that, and I want to assure you that we plan to work in full cooperation with your team once it arrives."

"My supervisor will appreciate that," Henry replied, his gaze never leaving Tessa. He had the bluest eyes she'd ever seen, and his lashes were dark brown and tipped with gold.

"How are you feeling, Tessa?" he asked, and

she knew it was only the first of many questions he planned to ask.

"Aside from a headache, fine," she replied, wishing she had the courage to tell all of them to leave the room. She needed some time to think things through, to make decisions about how much of her past she wanted to reveal.

Any of it felt like too much, but she was afraid they would dig for answers if she avoided questions.

Then again, maybe they wouldn't ask about anything except that night and the kidnapping.

"I'm glad. You risked a lot to help my daughter, and I want you to know how much I appreciate that." He was studying her face, his gaze stopping for a moment too long on the narrow white line that cut from her ear to her temple.

She tensed, waiting for him to ask how she'd gotten it.

Instead, he met her eyes again. "I owe you a lot."

"You don't owe me anything," she said, and she meant it.

"We'll have to agree to disagree." He grabbed a chair that was sitting against the wall and placed it in front of her.

She knew he planned to sit there. Too close for her to avoid his eyes.

"I really do have a headache," she murmured, hoping he would get the hint and leave.

"I won't take much of your time." He eyed the throbbing area on her temple. She'd seen herself in the mirror. What had felt like a glancing blow had left a huge knot and an ugly bruise. Apparently, that wasn't enough to dissuade him from questioning her.

He dropped into the chair, leaning toward her, his elbows on his knees, his gaze direct. "Tell me what happened this morning."

She repeated everything she'd told the police. She gave as many details as she could remember. The sunglasses. The pale skin. The dark hair. The gun.

He didn't interrupt, didn't cut in to ask for clarification. He didn't take notes. He just stared into her eyes, judging—she thought—her honesty.

Fortunately, she'd learned a lot during her years living with her mother. She had watched uniformed officers ask questions and watched her mother shift and squirm, trying to hide that she was strung out on drugs or hiding a few ounces of cocaine in her sleeve, or blouse or pants pocket.

Tessa kept still, kept focused, refused to look away.

Because, everything she was saying was the truth.

Only her identity was a lie.

Four months before she'd left Napa Valley,

she'd purchased a new identity from an old acquaintance. She had attended middle school with him, and she had known that her grandmother had offered him a place to stay when his stepfather had kicked him out. He had been happy to help Tessa. For a price. Eight months of saving every penny of the allowance Patrick gave her had made the purchase possible.

The day she'd left California, she had destroyed her driver's license and become Tessa Carlson. From that day forward, she had tried to convince herself she had never been anyone else.

By the time she finished speaking, she felt exhausted, the pain in her head a throbbing ache that made her want to close her eyes and sleep for a while.

"How about the Jeep, Tessa?" he prodded. "Did you notice anything about the interior that might help us?"

"I was a little too busy trying to figure out how to save myself and Everly to worry about the color of the seats or the vehicle identification number, Agent Miller."

"Call me Henry. Most people who save my daughter's life do."

"Do your daughters often need saving?" she asked, and he smiled.

"This is the first and, hopefully, last time."

"I'm glad I was in the right place at the right

time," she murmured, still refusing to look away from his unwavering gaze.

He had blue-gray eyes that reminded her of the fog that had often rolled across the vineyards in Napa Valley. She had liked to sit and watch it as the sun rose, wishing and hoping for changes that never came. Sometimes praying the way Hester had taught her, but never believing that God would hear the cries of a woman who had wandered so far from His truth.

It had taken many years and thousands of miles for her to understand the truth of God's love and forgiveness.

"We're all glad you were," the chief interjected, and she allowed herself to finally look away from Henry.

"You're a newcomer to Provincetown," the chief continued.

"I've been here for three years. That's not so new."

"You weren't raised here, is what I mean," he amended. "But that doesn't mean we don't think of you as part of the community. Your well-being during this investigation is paramount. Once you return home, I'll have patrols ride past your house every few hours."

"He wasn't trying to kidnap me, Chief Simpson. He was after Everly."

"Everly didn't see his face. You did," the

chief responded, the words chilling. She hadn't thought about what it meant to be the sole witness to a kidnapping attempt or to be the key witness in a crime that could put someone in jail for a very long time. She'd been too busy worrying about the past to think about the very clear and present danger she might be in.

"Do you really think he will come after me?" she asked.

"If I were in his shoes, I wouldn't. I'd leave Provincetown and never return."

"You're assuming he's not from the area," Kayla said.

The chief frowned. "I'm not assuming anything, officer. I'm saying that if I were in his shoes, I'd leave town and never return. I have no real idea what he might do. If I could figure out the minds of criminals, I'd be able to stop a lot of terrible things before they happened. I need to get back to town. The state police are bringing in their evidence team, and I'd like to be there when they arrive. Officer Delphina, you are to take station outside the door. Don't let anyone in who isn't on the list."

He strode into the hall, and Kayla and Officer Mitchel followed close behind.

That left Tessa and Henry.

Which shouldn't have bothered her, but did.

"Do you have more questions?" she asked,

picking at the tape that held a bandage on her left knee in place. She had insisted on staying in her street clothes, and her black slacks were torn at both knees, the fabric ripped away to reveal pale skin. The chief had arrived with her purse and her cell phone. Both had survived their time in the street. Her coat had been taken for forensic testing. The police were hoping to find a hair from the kidnapper on it. Betty's coat was lying across a table near the far wall.

Focusing on those things did not keep her from noticing how quiet Henry had become. How still and watchful he was.

He seemed to be waiting for something, and she had no idea what.

She tore at the tape again, and he pulled her hand away.

She winced, jerking back reflexively, her cheeks hot with embarrassment when she realized what she'd done.

"You're nervous," he commented, and she looked up, saw that he was watching her with a mixture of what she thought was curiosity and suspicion.

"After what Chief Simpson said, who wouldn't be?"

"You were nervous before that."

He was right, and she wasn't going to pretend otherwise. "I'm not used to having four law-enforcement officers questioning me while I sit on a hospital bed."

"I don't think many people are."

"Look, Henry, I've told you everything I know about what happened today, and—"

"You haven't told me everything," he interrupted.

"Of course I have."

"You haven't told me why you fled the scene when the police arrived."

There it was.

A question she didn't have a good answer to.

If she had been given time alone, she might have been able to think of one.

"I was in shock." That seemed to be as good a reason as any.

"Most people who are in shock don't wander away from help."

"I'm not most people," she replied, standing and walking to the door. She had nowhere to go. The hospital was an hour's drive from Provincetown, and she had no car. She was stuck until Ernie and Betty arrived.

"No, I guess you're not." He was on his feet, watching her as she opened the door and glanced into the hall. Kayla was leaning against the wall, reading a magazine. She smiled when she saw Tessa.

"Everything okay?"

"I'm just getting antsy. Betty and Ernie said they were coming. When they get here, you'll let them in, right?"

"Of course," she responded.

"Thanks. I'm tired. I may nap while I'm waiting, and I don't want to miss them," she said, hoping Henry would get the hint and leave the room.

"Good thinking." Kayla's gaze dropped to the magazine. A white fluffy dress on the back cover screamed that it was bridal.

"Are you engaged, Kayla?" Tessa asked, suddenly curious. They'd known each other for a few years. They attended the same church. Kayla ate meals at the diner several times a week, but Tessa couldn't call her a friend.

She couldn't really call anyone that.

"Not yet, but I'm hopeful. The big three-oh is coming up, and I'm not getting any younger. I'd like to have a few babies before the clock stops ticking." She smiled and met Tessa's eyes. "My boyfriend is a professor at Boston University. He teaches Tuesday and Thursday and comes down on Friday and Saturday. It's working for now."

"Will you move there after you are married?"

"No. I left the city life for good. Nathan knows that. What about you? Any wedding bells in the future? I've got more of these where this one came from." She gave the magazine a quick shake and smiled.

"I left the relationship life for good. Every guy who's asked me out knows that."

Kayla laughed. "You say that now, but we never know what God will do."

"No. I guess we don't. I'd better get that nap," she said, shutting down the conversation before it could get more personal. She'd already said too much. She'd given Kayla a glimpse into a past she never talked about.

Worse, Henry was standing behind her, probably listening to every word.

She ducked back into the room and whirled around.

He was near the window, the curtains pulled back so that watery sunlight poured into the room.

"See anything interesting?" she asked.

"A few dark-colored Jeeps," he said, his words leaving her cold.

She walked toward the window, but he motioned for her to stay back. "Let's not give him an easy target."

"We're three stories up."

"If he has an assault rifle, that distance won't matter."

She stepped back, nearly stumbling over a chair in her haste to get out of the line of fire and knocking over a small table that held a nearly empty roll of surgical tape and a totally empty pitcher a nurse had offered to fill with water.

She scooped up both, then set the table upright and put the pitcher and tape on top of it, knowing that Henry was watching.

She didn't meet his eyes, didn't acknowledge what he'd said or her own rising fear.

This was not what she'd planned for her day. It wasn't what she'd planned for her life. She'd graduated from high school at sixteen and earned a partial scholarship to the local community college. She'd worked three jobs to pay the rest of her tuition.

Patrick had walked into the high-end restaurant where she waited tables the night she'd turned eighteen. He'd heard it was her birthday and had left a beautiful bracelet as a tip. He had been nearly twenty years older, suave, sophisticated and more than capable of sweeping a world-weary street kid off her feet.

She'd fallen for the promises he's whispered in her ear.

She'd believed every pretty lie he'd told her.

She'd given up her jobs, her classes, her scholarships.

She didn't want to give up more.

She didn't want to leave her cozy cottage in

Provincetown and begin again somewhere else, but she was terrified that it would be necessary.

The woman she'd been in Napa Valley had disappeared.

Tessa could do the same.

If she had to.

Within three hours of being admitted to the hospital, Everly was awake and on the move. She bounced from one side of the room to the other, chattering endlessly.

Henry suspected nerves were driving her motormouth.

She'd been disoriented and afraid when she'd woken, nervous about the hospital, the police officer and the nurse.

He'd reassured her as best he could, and then he'd let Aria distract her. The two were currently singing praise songs at the top of their lungs. Like their mother, they could each carry a tune, and like her, they loved to belt out whatever song popped into their heads.

Diane would have had a blast making music with the girls.

The thought didn't make him as sad as it once had. The pain of losing her had become a dull ache compared to the searing agony he'd once felt.

"Girls, how about you lower your voices?" he suggested.

"Why?" Everly asked, spinning in circles, her braided hair flying behind her.

She'd almost become a terrible statistic. He didn't think he'd ever be able to look at her without remembering that, and he knew he would never be able to remember without thanking God it hadn't happened.

Tessa had said she had been in the right place at the right time. God had orchestrated that. Henry believed that the same way he believed that the sun would set and rise again.

He also believed that Tessa was hiding something.

He'd listened to her statement of the morning's events. He'd watched her face. He had looked into her eyes. He felt certain she had been telling the truth about the kidnapping, but he also felt certain she had not been honest about her reason for leaving the scene.

Not that she'd given a reason.

She'd said she had been in shock.

That sounded more like an excuse to him.

He hadn't pushed. She'd been pale, the bruise on her head deep purple. She had needed rest, and he had left the room so she could get it. Once she did, he'd question her again.

"Yes, Daddy, why? The Bible says to make a joyful noise. It does not say to do it quietly," Aria said.

"You can make joyful noises quietly. And because I asked you to, and because we're inside. You should be using your inside voices."

"Your father is right, dear," Rachelle said. "You're both being much too loud, and Nana is getting a headache."

"I'm getting a headache, too," Everly said.

Henry would have thought she was saying it to get attention, but she looked pale, her eyes shadowed.

"Why don't you lie down for a while, then, honey?"

"I want to lie down in my bed at Nana and Pop-pop's house," she responded, dropping onto the floor, the hospital gown pooling around her. "Why do we have to stay here?"

"The doctor wants to keep an eye on you for a while longer."

"The doctor could keep an eye on me at home, couldn't he?"

"It's a long drive, hotshot," Brett said. "The doctor can't make house calls that far from the hospital. What if people at the hospital got sick while he was too far away to help them?"

"The people at the hospital *are* sick, Pop-pop," Aria pointed out. "But, Everly isn't. Except for her headache, and I can take care of that. I know how to do it." She sat next to her twin and wrapped her arm around her.

"Sweetheart," Henry began.

"But I know why you don't want us to go home. That bad man might be there," Aria whispered so softly he almost didn't hear.

Shocked, Henry sat beside her and pulled her into his lap. "What bad man?"

"The one who came in the house and took my sister."

"What do you know about that?" he asked, wondering if she could have woken and seen the kidnapping and been too afraid to say anything.

"I heard Nana yelling about it in the phone. And then I heard Pop-pop telling Pastor Brendan Walker that we needed a lot of prayer because my sister was kidnapped."

"I am so sorry, Henry. I thought she was still sleeping," Rachelle said, her eyes moist with tears. She looked as pale and tired as Everly, and even Aria looked exhausted.

The hospital was a good place for the sick, but not for two little girls who'd been traumatized.

"Tell you what," he said. "How about I talk to the doctor and see if we can break out of this place? We can stop on the way home and pick up some hamburgers and fries. You girls can watch a movie while you eat it."

"We can watch a movie?" Everly asked, perking up enough to ease some of his concern.

"I don't see why not. It's the weekend, and tomorrow is your mother's birthday. We always do special things to celebrate that."

"We get to watch a movie," Everly whispered loudly in Aria's ear.

"But what about the bad guy?" Aria responded.

"I didn't see a bad guy," Everly said. "I think he was a figment."

"A what?" Brett asked, digging into a large bag he and Rachelle had brought.

"A figment. Like when I think I see the Loch Ness Monster in the bay, and you tell me that I'm seeing a figment."

"A figment of your imagination," Brett responded as he pulled a pair of pink jeans and a thick sweater from the bag.

"Right. That's what I think he was, so we're not going to worry anymore. Okay, Aria?"

Aria nodded, but she didn't seem convinced.

"We're not going to worry," Everly repeated, putting both her hands on her sister's cheeks and looking into her eyes. "We're going to eat French fries and watch a movie, and we're going to be happy, because it's almost Mommy's birthday."

"It is almost her birthday," Aria said. "I picked those clothes out for you. I gave you my pink jeans, because yours are dirty." She pointed to the outfit Brett held.

"You're the best sister. Come on. Let's go

in the bathroom, so I can change in privacy." Everly grabbed the clothes and marched away.

Aria followed more slowly, her feet shuffling and her shoulders sloped.

She hadn't forgotten what she'd heard, and Henry wasn't going to pretend that she didn't have good reason to worry.

"Aria," he said. "We're going to make sure you and Everly are safe. I promise."

"I think I have an idea about that, Daddy." She looked at him, her eyes so much like Diana's his chest hurt with it.

"What's that, sweetie?"

"We can get a dog. A big one that will bark when bad guys come around. I'll train him all by myself. So, he will lick good guys and bite bad guys."

"Dogs are great, and I'm sure you'd do a great job training one, but I'm not sure we have time," he hedged. The girls had been begging for a puppy for a year, and he'd been saying no for just as long. Even with Brett and Rachelle's help, life was hectic. He barely had time to do the daily chores. Adding a dog into the mix would only complicate things.

"Pop-pop said Mommy always wanted a dog when she was little, and his biggest regret was that he never let her get one, because he and Nana thought they were too busy."

Henry glanced at Brett.

"I guess I did say that. We were watching one of those dog movies the kids love, and it slipped out. I'm starting to think I need to wear a muzzle when I'm around my granddaughters." He shook his head. "Those little pitchers have very big ears."

"But the dog may be a good idea," Rachelle said after Aria disappeared into the bathroom. "I've heard they're a better deterrent than security alarms, and…" She lowered her voice to a whisper. "I am feeling a little nervous about going home."

"Chief Simpson promised round-the-clock protection," Brett said.

"Did he?" Henry asked. He hadn't been included in that conversation, and he would like to have been. He might be the father of the kidnapping victim, but he was also an FBI agent who was as desperate to stop the perp as Simpson.

"Yes. He said that between the local police, the FBI and the state police, we'll be well-protected. He's worried, and I am, too. I've lived a good long life. If something happened to me, that would be okay, but if something happened to—"

"Brett, stop," Rachelle said. "Nothing is going to happen to any of us. We're going to live many more years and watch the girls grow up and be there when they marry, and maybe even see our first great-grandchild."

"How about we don't talk about the girls having babies until they're not babies anymore?" Henry suggested, glancing at his phone as a text came through. Wren had arrived. She and Jessica were heading to the room.

If the perp who had tried to take Everly *was* the serial kidnapper, he'd made his first and last mistake. He had allowed himself to be seen by a witness—Tessa—who was able and willing to identify him.

All they needed was a name and a face to put in a lineup.

Someone knocked, the hard, quick rap almost frantic. The door flew open and the officer who'd been guarding Tessa's room charged in. "Is she here?"

"Who?"

"Tessa!"

"She's supposed to be upstairs. In her room."

"I'm well aware of where she's supposed to be," the officer snapped. "I had to intervene in an altercation between two patients. When I returned to the room, she was gone."

"Did you contact Security?"

"Of course, I did. They should have put the hospital on lockdown."

"I didn't hear an announcement. Call again.

And, don't leave my daughters alone in this room!" he nearly shouted as he darted out of the room.

The hallway was almost empty, the stairwell silent as he entered it and bounded up the flight of stairs. He planned to run to Tessa's room, see if he could figure out the path she'd taken, but something on the stairs caught his attention. A piece of surgical tape had been dropped in the center tread of one of the steps heading to the fourth floor.

Another was two steps above it, lying near the baseboard on the landing. Aside from those two pieces of tape, the stairwell was free of debris or litter.

He'd seen surgical tape in Tessa's room.

He'd watched her pick it up and set in on the table she'd knocked over. Was it possible she'd grabbed it and was trying to leave a trail?

If so, it was a short one.

And, it was leading up.

# FOUR

Tessa hadn't learned much from her mother, but she *had* learned how to fight. From her grandmother, she'd learned everything else—how to cook, to clean, to be respectful.

How to take turns, to wait and to be patient.

She was using those last two skills now, biding her time as she was dragged up another flight of stairs by the man who'd forced her from her hospital room at gunpoint.

He had it pointed at her side as they ascended, the barrel snagging on her shirt as they sprinted upward.

She reached in her pocket, trying to tear off more of the surgical tape she'd snagged from the table as he'd rushed her from her room.

She wasn't sure what she had thought she could do with it. Leaving a trail like Hansel and Gretel didn't seem like a good plan for staying alive. Currently, though, it was the only plan she had.

"What are you doing?" the man growled, his light-eyed gaze dropping to her pocket, his red hair standing in wild tufts around his head. He was on something. She recognized the signs. If she played it smart, she might be able to use that to her advantage.

Then again, her mother had always been paranoid when she'd been high. It might be more difficult than she hoped to find an opportunity to escape someone in that condition.

"Nothing," she responded, keeping her hand in her pocket and continuing upward. They would reach the door to the roof soon. She wasn't sure what he planned to do to her once they were there, but she didn't think it would be anything good.

"What's in your pocket?"

"Just this." She pulled out the tape, because she didn't want to give him an excuse to search for it.

He snatched it from her hand and tossed it away.

It rolled down the steps and stopped on the lower landing.

"There. Now, we don't have to worry about that anymore, do we?" he sneered, jerking her up the next few steps, the gun still pressed to her side.

"We wouldn't have to worry about anything, if you would let me go," she responded.

"Sorry, lady. I can't."

"Why not? I haven't done anything to you. I don't even know you."

"This isn't about what you know. It's about money. I need some. Some guy offered me and my buddies some." He shrugged, the gun slipping a fraction of an inch away. "Here we are."

"What guy?"

"You ask a lot of questions for someone who has a gun pointed at her heart."

It was now pointed at her hip, but she didn't point that out to him. "If I'm going to die, I'd like to know why."

"Who said you were going to die?"

"You have a gun. You're taking me up to the roof. I can't see this ending any other way." She shuddered, trying to drag her feet as they passed the seventh-floor landing and headed toward the fire door that led to the roof. It was an emergency exit, and she prayed the alarm would sound as they moved through.

That might be the distraction she needed to knock the gun from his hand and escape.

"You have a point, but if you think I'm planning to shoot you, you're wrong. This is going to be a suicide."

"It is?"

"Sure. You got knocked on the head. You got confused about your life, and you decided to end it. You waltzed up to the roof and took a header over the side of it."

"You actually think people are going to believe I killed myself?"

"I don't see why not. Those football players with the concussions do it."

"How much were you offered to do this? I'll offer you more," she said, hoping that greed might motivate him to release her.

"Nice trick, lady, but I'm not falling for it. If you offer to pay me, and I accept, you'll be on the phone with the police as soon as I let you go."

"No, I won't. I won't tell anybody about our bargain."

"Of course you won't. You'll be dead," he replied coldly, his nearly colorless eyes raking her from head to toe.

"I mean, if you let me live."

"I know what you meant. I don't really care what you meant. I'm being paid good money, and I can't see turning on the person who's paying me. If I do, I could end up with a price on my head."

He shoved his hand against the crash bar of the door, but it didn't open.

The door didn't open.

He tried again, the gun slipping from Tessa's side as he shoved his weight against the metal bar, his wild cursing covering what sounded like someone ascending the stairs.

Tessa didn't dare glance down and call attention to what she'd heard.

"They locked it," he muttered. "They probably put the whole place on lockdown. I should have had my buddies kill that cop to make certain she kept her big mouth shut."

"We can still get up to the roof. I've picked locks before," Tessa said. "Do you have a credit card or…?"

He backhanded her, and she flew against the door, stars dancing in her periphery as she slid to the floor.

"I guess your death doesn't have to be a suicide for me to get paid." He raised the gun and pointed it at her head. "Sorry about this. I'm not much for killing, but a man has to do what a man has to—"

She lunged for his knees, throwing her weight into his legs and sending him crashing down the stairs. The gun exploded, the bullet ricocheting off the metal door and slamming into Tessa's shoulder.

She barely felt it.

She was too busy crab-crawling down the

stairs in pursuit of the gun that had clattered to the landing below.

She almost made it.

She was steps away, trying to get to her feet, dizzy from the blood that was oozing down her arm.

The gunman righted himself and charged toward her, hands out and face red with fury.

She screamed, kicking him in the stomach as he fell on top of her, his hands around her throat.

A million memories filled her head—Patrick throwing a vase, knocking her down, straddling her body with his hands around her throat.

How many times had she lived through this?

She wasn't going to die at the hands of a stranger when she'd survived the violence of a man who'd claimed to love her.

Was she?

*Please, God, don't let me die.*

She clawed at his hands, darkness edging in.

And then he was gone, lifted away and slammed against the wall.

People were calling out, hollering through the once-silent stairwell, and she was lying on the steps, staring at the ceiling, blood seeping from her shoulder, her ears still ringing from the gun's report.

"You're going to be okay," someone said, and she realized Henry was kneeling beside her, his eyes more gray than blue, his hands gentle as he pulled fabric away from the bullet wound.

"Where is he?" she replied, pushing his hand away and sitting. She felt woozy and grabbed his arm, holding herself steady as she tried to find the gunman in the crowd of people.

"Handcuffed and heading down the stairs."

"He said he had friends. He said something about having them kill Kayla."

"They've been apprehended."

"Someone hired him. It had to have been the kidnapper."

"I know," he responded. "We're going to question him, see when he was hired, and where. Hopefully, the kidnapper is still hanging around."

"Is Everly okay? They didn't try to get to her, did they?" she asked.

"Tessa, we have everything under control. I promise you that."

"Then why does it feel like everything is out of control?" she asked, her teeth chattering, her body shaking. She felt cold to the bone. Colder than she ever had before.

"Because you're scared," he replied.

"I'm not scared. I'm terrified," she responded. She thought he smiled, but a doctor shoved in beside him and pressed a thick pad of gauze against the wound.

"I think it's just a flesh wound," Tessa said. "So, if you don't mind, I'd like to go home."

"You're going to be fine, but you're not going home. Not yet," the doctor said.

She wanted to argue, but her eyes drifted closed.

When she opened them again, she was on a gurney being rushed through the hospital corridor. Henry was jogging beside her, holding her hand and talking to a tall stunning woman dressed in a black suit and pale purple blouse.

"What's going on?" Tessa asked, and the woman responded.

"You're going to surgery."

"I don't think I need surgery."

"Based on the amount of blood you're losing, I'd say you do," Henry replied grimly.

"But, I really think I'm okay," she said, or tried to say—her mind was fuzzy and the world spinning.

"Hun?" a nurse said, leaning down so she could look in her eyes. "Is there anyone you want me to call? Family? Friends?"

She wanted there to be.

She did.

She wanted to know that someone was waiting for her, praying for her, anxiously waiting to see her when she was finally out of surgery.

But the only people she could think of were

Betty and Ernie, and they were her bosses. Not her friends.

"No," she responded, and she saw the pity in the nurse's eyes as she was wheeled through the double doors that led into the operating theater.

Henry waited until the double doors closed, and then turned to face Wren Santino. She'd arrived at the hospital just as the chaos had begun and had sent Jessica to protect the girls and his in-laws while she assisted in locating and freeing Tessa.

Despite their race upstairs, she didn't have a wrinkle in her suit or hair out of place.

"I want this guy caught. Today," he said, somehow keeping rage from seeping into his voice.

"We all do, but anger isn't the way to make it happen," she responded.

"Who said I'm angry?"

"Aren't you?"

"Yes," he admitted.

"I don't blame you, but it's not going to change what happened. The kidnapper hired a few thugs to do what he couldn't. They almost managed it. Those are facts. The other fact is, they didn't. Tessa is going to be okay."

"And, if we can get them to talk, we may get an even better description of our kidnapper."

"They'll talk. Eventually. For now, we're going to put safety nets in place. We're going to make certain your family is protected. We're going to make certain Tessa is. We're going to continue our hunt for the kidnapper. Today or tomorrow or the next day. Eventually, we'll find him."

"Eventually isn't good enough when the guy has already kidnapped and victimized five little girls."

"Yesterday wouldn't have been good enough. No day except the day before he kidnapped his first victim would be. But achieving that would be impossible, so we're going to focus on doing what we can."

"Right. What's the plan?"

"How about we send your in-laws and Jessica back to their place? You and I can go to the local precinct and have a chat with the guy who shot Tessa."

"And leave her here without any protection?"

"She's in surgery. There are police officers in the lobby, and we'll make sure there are several assigned to escort her from surgery to recover in her room."

It was a good plan. In theory.

In actuality, he didn't like it.

There'd been police and security guards all

over the hospital when Tessa was abducted from her room.

"I'd feel better sticking around and keeping an eye on things myself," he said.

Wren looked surprised, but didn't argue. "That's fine. I'll go to the precinct, and I'll give you a call if we get any helpful information."

"Thanks."

"Let's both save our thanks until we have this guy behind bars. I'll go down to Everly's room and let Jessica know what's going on. You want me to have the girls come up here to say goodbye?"

"Sure," he responded.

"All right. They should be up in a few minutes. I'm heading out as soon as I fill Jessica in. If anything comes up, call."

"I will," he said as she walked away.

The corridor fell silent, and he dropped into a chair that sat against the wall. It had been a long morning for all of them, and he wanted to make sure the girls were still doing okay. He also wanted to make sure Tessa stayed okay. The gunman hadn't been hired to kidnap Everly. He'd been hired to silence her rescuer.

Tess was the one in real and immediate danger. Not the girls.

As much as he wanted to escort the girls home, go to the Provincetown Police Department and question the gunman and his friends, he was more concerned about keeping Tessa safe.

She'd risked her life for his daughter.

He wasn't going to let her lose it.

Eventually, they'd find the kidnapper. For now, she was his top priority.

All's well that ends well.

That's what his mother used to say when things got tough and the electricity or water were turned off for the umpteenth time or they had empty cupboards for the second day in a row. As soon as she scraped together enough money from her two jobs to pay the bills or buy the food or fix the old car their landlord had given her, she'd smile and say that all was well that ended well.

She'd died four years before the girls were born, her body ravaged by cancer, but her joy still firmly in place.

*All's well that ends well, and this will end well for me. No matter what the earthly outcome.* She'd whispered that as she was lying on her deathbed, and he'd known she'd believed it. She'd had the strongest faith of any person he'd ever met, her love for the things of God overshadowing all that she said and did. She'd raised him alone when his father had walked out and filed for divorce. Henry had been three. Much too young to remember anything about the man. As far as he knew, his mother had never received a dime of child support. He couldn't recall ever getting a card or a phone call from the man whose surname he shared. His mother had gotten pregnant at sixteen, married at seventeen and had been a divorced single mother by the time she'd turned twenty. She'd never complained, though. She'd worked hard. She'd done the best she could with what she had.

And she had really believed everything would always turn out okay.

He wanted to be the same. He liked to believe his faith was as strong as hers. That, no matter what, he could look at his life and say *all is well that ends well*.

But things wouldn't have been fine if Everly had disappeared. Things wouldn't be fine if Tessa died because she had kept that from happening.

That was the truth.

His truth, anyway.

Tessa had said she was okay, but he'd seen the bullet hole and the blood pulsing out of it. It had gone straight into her shoulder and probably hit the bone. She'd have a long recovery ahead, and Henry didn't plan on letting her face it alone. He'd heard her response when the nurse had asked if she had family. For whatever reason, she was alone in the world. Or, had been.

Now, she had him and his family.

They'd make certain that she recovered, that her medical bills were paid and that she didn't suffer financially while she was rehabbing.

It was the least they could do for her.

That and make sure she was safe, that the man who'd been slipping under the radar, hunting in the darkest hours of the morning and stealing children from the safety of their homes, didn't do what his hired thugs had attempted—silence her.

# FIVE

Tessa walked to the diner her first day back at work.

Not because she had to. Because she wanted to prove that she could.

She left the house the same way she had four weeks prior—dressed in her winter coat, the diner key in her back pocket, her purse slung over her shoulder. She checked the lock twice before she stepped onto the path and hurried through the quiet streets, her heart pounding double time, her mind flashing back to that moment when she'd seen Everly being kidnapped.

It was almost enough to make her return home, but she'd promised herself that she wouldn't live in fear. The three men who had been apprehended at the hospital had insisted they didn't know who had hired them. They'd refused to give a description. They'd refused to cooperate with the police. All three had been booked on charges of attempted murder. All three would stay in prison until their trials.

That didn't make her feel safer.

Neither did Henry's assurance that the kidnapper had left the Cape and was on the run. The Jeep he'd used during the attempted kidnapping had been located in New Hampshire three days after Tessa had been shot. The police had dusted for prints and pulled several that they hoped would get a hit in the national data banks. They'd also been able to pull two sources of DNA off a gun they'd found beneath the seat. One was Tessa's. The other DNA belonged to an unknown male. They were running that through national data banks as well. Henry said they were even working with several DNA-ancestry companies to see if there were potential matches there.

It would take time, but he seemed confident they would find the kidnapper.

She hoped so.

But while she waited, she refused to live in fear.

At least not fear of the kidnapper.

If she was honest, she'd admit she was still afraid of Patrick.

In the weeks following the kidnapping, there'd been a buzz of media attention. Tessa had been offered thousands of dollars to give interviews and appear on live news programs.

She'd refused all the offers.

As soon as she'd been released from the hospital, she'd locked herself in the cottage, and she'd stayed there until most of the furor had blown over. As far as she knew, the only picture that had been leaked to the media was of a photo that hung in the diner—Tessa holding her employee-of-the-month award two years ago. In it, she looked nothing like the woman who'd left Napa Valley. She'd let her hair go back to its natural mousy color. She'd stopped wearing the violet-colored contacts that Patrick had loved. Instead of the short, trendy hairstyle she'd paid hundreds of dollars for, she'd had her hair pulled back in a ponytail, a fringe of bangs hanging over her eyes.

She'd seen the photo on the nightly news while she was recovering from surgery. The next day, it had made national headlines. Since then, she'd been telling herself that Patrick would never recognize her as the dowdy waitress in the fuzzy photo.

Every night, she prayed that she was right.

Every night, she checked the locks on her windows and doors and lay in bed for hours listening to the creaks and groans of the settling house. She'd drift off to sleep and wake from nightmares. Not of the kidnapping or the attack in the hospital. Of Patrick, his hands around her throat, strangling the life from her.

She needed to move on. Just like she had when she'd left Napa Valley. Put the fear behind her and take control of her life again.

Walking to work was the first step in that, but winter had settled hard, and she was shivering by the time she reached Rachelle and Brett Halifax's street, her toes numb in her rubber-soled black sneakers. There was light shining in a first-floor window of their house, and she wondered if the girls were there for the weekend. They usually were, and the fact that Tessa knew that bothered her.

She'd woken from surgery expecting to be alone.

Instead, Henry had been beside her, sitting in a chair, reading a Gideon Bible. He'd offered her ice chips, asked if she was in pain, called the nurse when she'd said she was.

Since then, he and his family had made themselves part of her life. They'd brought her meals, cleaned her house, called her in the evening when the sun was going down and the shadows were getting long. The girls would giggle into the receiver, and Tessa would not be able to keep herself from smiling.

Somehow, the twins had found their way into her heart.

She was fine with that.

She'd never thought of herself as maternal, but she loved painting fingernails and helping the girls choose outfits for church. Twice, she'd had Saturday-night dinner at the Halifax place. Brett had cooked wonderful meals while the girls chattered endlessly about school and friends. Everly was the boisterous one. Aria the quieter, more thoughtful twin. Both were lovely well-mannered girls who were obviously deeply loved by their family. Rachelle had shown Tessa photos of the girls' mother—a beautiful black-haired woman who had been a teacher in the inner city, a person devoted to helping the less fortunate. Someone Tessa knew she would have liked.

The same way she liked Rachelle and Brett and the girls.

The same way she liked Henry.

And that, she knew, was the root of her unease regarding the family. Not the twins. Not the Halifaxes. Henry.

He'd been at the dinners, sharing stories of the girls' antics and asking questions that Tessa hadn't been able to answer. At least not completely. She'd told him the truth about her childhood—about her mother's drug problems, and her grandmother's more positive influence.

She'd shared bits and pieces from her young adult years, mentioning Patrick in passing but not providing his surname, his occupation, or where he'd lived.

When Henry pressed for more details, she sidestepped the questions or changed the subject.

She knew he noticed, and there was a huge part of her that wanted to tell him everything.

That scared her.

Not because she was afraid of what he'd think or say or do, but because, in the time she'd lived in Provincetown, she'd never been tempted to share her story with anyone.

She frowned, her gaze shifting to the Halifax place.

It was the antithesis of every home she'd ever shared—warm and welcoming, nurturing and wholesome. She longed to be part of that, but being part of anything under false pretenses was wrong. And, she supposed, a false identity was the same.

She sighed, shoving her hands in her pockets to try to warm them.

"It's an awfully cold day to be out walking," a man said, and she whirled around, saw Henry standing beneath the streetlight near his in-laws' driveway.

"You scared me," she said, her heart racing for reasons that had nothing to do with terror.

"I'm sorry about that. I was sitting on the porch when you walked by. I thought you'd seen me."

"I would have said hello if I had," she replied as he walked toward her.

"Would you have?" he asked, shrugging out of his coat and wrapping it around her shoulders.

"Is there a reason you think I wouldn't?" she responded, the scent of pine needles and wood fires drifting in the air.

"There you go again. Answering a question with a question."

"And there you go, asking more questions than I want to answer," she replied. She slipped the coat from her shoulders, ignoring the twinge in her bad arm as she handed it back to him. "You're going to freeze out here without a coat."

"According to Rachelle, you were going to freeze on your way to work," he said.

"Is she the reason you were sitting on the porch?"

"You did tell her that you planned to walk to work today."

"We had lunch together yesterday."

"That's what she said. Brett is in Boston teaching at a medical seminar, and he has their car. Since she doesn't have a vehicle, Rachelle decided to hand you hot chocolate and a blanket on your way past. She laid out the plan when I arrived with the girls last night."

"You talked her out of it?"

"She's seventy. I didn't want her waking up before dawn to do something I could easily handle. I promised I'd waylay you and drive you the rest of the way to Ernie's. So, here I am." He smiled, taking her arm and leading her back to the Halifaxes' place. "My SUV warms up quickly. Hop in. I'll crank up the heat."

He opened the door, and she did as he asked, telling herself that this was no different than any other time she'd been in the SUV with him. Since her surgery, he'd driven her to doctor's appointments and physical-therapy sessions, taking time off from work to be there on several occasions.

It had felt odd to have someone inconvenience himself for her sake. Aside from Hester, there'd been no one in Tessa's life who would willingly do that. Her past relationships had always been inequitable, and she'd often burned out in her efforts to make the other person happy. In Los Angeles and Napa Valley, relationships had been difficult and fraught with tension and violence.

With Henry, things were easy.

She wasn't sure what to make of that, or how to respond.

Heat poured from the vents as he pulled out of

the driveway, and she held her hands in front of them, warming her fingers. Henry didn't complain, didn't demand that she sit still, didn't call her a silly little twit who should have known better than to walk in fifteen-degree weather. He hummed along with the radio, his fingers tapping the leather steering wheel.

"Is this what it's supposed to be like?" she asked, the words slipping out before she could think better of them.

"What?" he asked, taking the turn onto Commercial Street slowly. If he was bothered by the fact that Rachelle had convinced him to get up at the crack of dawn to drive Tessa to work, he didn't show it.

"Friendship? Companionship? Is it supposed to be this easy? Not that I'm saying we're friends or companions. I know you're just doing these things because I helped your daughter. I'm just curious. I've never—"

"You haven't let me answer the question," he said quietly as he pulled up to the curb in front of the diner.

"Sorry," she responded, embarrassed because she'd asked, and because she couldn't seem to stop her verbal spewing. She spent hours every day with strangers, making small talk as she took orders and served meals. It seemed silly to get nervous while she was talking to Henry, but that's how she felt.

He put the SUV in Park and shifted to face her, his eyes silvery blue in the dashboard light. "I think that a good friendship *is* easy and comfortable, but not like a worn shoe or a threadbare and pilled blanket. Like a familiar song or the patter of rain on a tin roof. It's the kind of thing a person can come back to again and again and never be bored with. It's familiar, and yet, somehow, always brand-new."

"That's very…poetic," she murmured, a lump in her throat because it hadn't just been poetic, it had been beautiful. She'd never had that kind of friendship. As a child, she'd had a few pals that she'd walked to school with. Most of them had left the projects or joined local gangs when they entered middle school. Eventually, Tessa had decided to go it alone. To do as her grandmother had suggested and mind her business, take the path of kindness and avoid the troublemakers of the world.

She'd done a good job of that.

Until she'd met Patrick.

"You didn't know I had a little poetry in me, huh?" he asked, offering a half smile that made her pulse jump.

"You seem more the rock-climbing, outdoor type," she replied, and his smile broadened.

"I am. When I was a kid, I used to camp under the stars. If it got chilly, I'd build a fire and listen to it crackle and spit in the darkness."

"Were you a Scout?"

"I was a dirt-poor country boy," he replied. "My mother and I lived in a single-wide trailer on the edge of a defunct farm. Cheap rent and an understanding landlord who never once evicted us, but hot as Hades in the summer and stuffy and dank in the winter. Sleeping outside was preferable."

"What about your dad?"

"He left when I was three. I've seen a couple pictures of the house he and my mother shared. It wasn't much better than the trailer." His smile had faded but there wasn't any self-pity or embarrassment in his voice. Why would there be? He'd come from nothing and made it into the FBI. He had nice suits and polished shoes. The girls had clean clothes, plenty of toys and lots of love.

"What you've accomplished is incredible. Your mother must be very proud of you."

"She passed away before the girls were born, but she was definitely a proud mama. The year I graduated college, I was able to rent her a place in a nice apartment complex. Brand-new appliances, hot and cold water, heat and cooling systems. She loved it. She also loved to brag about my degree and my job in law enforcement. We had a couple of great Christmases there. The last Christmas we spent together, she cooked the meal. The turkey was awful, but the joy was real. Diane and I had just gotten married, and we spent Christmas day with Mom." He looked softer when he spoke of his family, and Tessa's heart ached with longing for the kind of relationship that put that expression on someone's face—fondness, admiration and respect, all gleaming from the gentle-eyed gaze of the one remembering.

But, of course, she would never have anything close, because she could never tell the truth about who she was, where she had come from or what she had done to leave the past behind.

"I had better get inside. Ernie likes the diner a certain way before it opens, and I need to prove that I can still manage that," she murmured, her voice husky with useless emotion.

She wasn't going to cry over what she couldn't have.

She wasn't going to mourn a silly dream.

She opened the SUV door, frigid air sweeping in and cooling her hot cheeks.

"You didn't let me finish." Henry grabbed her hand before she could exit the vehicle. His grip was loose, but the connection between them so strong she couldn't make herself pull away.

"Finish what?"

"Answering your question."

"I thought you had."

"Not quite." He tucked a strand of hair behind her ear, his fingers drifting across the thin scar that disappeared into her hairline. "You said I was doing this because of what you did for Everly. I wanted to tell you that my being here this morning has nothing to do with that."

"Then, what does it have to do with?"

"You."

That one word made her pulse jump and her heart ache.

She wanted to believe it was the truth. That he hadn't driven her to the diner because he had some false sense of obligation, or some erroneous belief that he needed to balance the scales. "You shouldn't say things like that, Henry."

"Why not? I have the girls and my in-laws, and I'm grateful for that, but it's nice to add to my small circle of friends."

"Your circle of friends isn't small. Everyone in Provincetown knows you." She'd noticed that when they'd gone to doctor's appointments or taken the girls for walks on the beach together. People always called Henry's name, greeting him and the girls as if they were old friends.

They probably were. She'd heard the stories about Diane and how much she'd loved the

Cape. This had been the family's favorite place to spend time together. Henry had been visiting the huge Victorian and the quaint town since he'd met Diane during their junior year of college. She knew all that because she listened. Not because she asked.

"The circle of people that I would trust with my daughters is tiny. You're in it. That means something to me. You mean something to me, and not just because you saved Everly's life."

The words were sweet, and she wanted to believe them, but she'd been swept up in pretty words before—she'd allowed herself to believe in things that weren't true.

She'd sworn that she'd never repeat the mistake.

"That's nice of you to say, Henry. I appreciate it."

"But, you don't believe it?" he raised a sandy eyebrow, and she could see the questions in his eyes.

"We've been tossed into this together, but eventually you'll find the man who kidnapped Everly. Once you do, we'll go our separate ways again."

"Is that what you're hoping?"

"It's a fact. People meet. People connect. People walk away."

"Sometimes, they don't."

"Do you have any updates on the DNA results?" she asked, changing the subject and not caring that it was obvious. She didn't want to talk about what might be, because she was afraid to believe in it. Afraid of being hurt again.

His jaw tightened, his eyes flashing with something that looked like irritation. "You are very good at sidestepping things."

"Does that mean you don't have an update?"

"We do. That was the other reason I wanted to talk to you this morning. One of the ancestry businesses we contacted has a potential match."

"So, you know his name?" she asked, excited by the possibility, hopeful that she could finally put to rest any concerns that the kidnapper would come after her.

"Not yet. We subpoenaed the company and got a name, but the DNA match is showing as a distant male relative."

"Which means what? A cousin?"

"Or an uncle. We're doing some research, trying to find someone in the family tree who matches the criminal profile Jessica worked up."

"White male. Twenty-five to forty. Professional. Well-educated," she said, repeating what she'd been told, and he nodded.

"And someone who has a job in the medical field."

"I didn't realize that was part of it."

"It wasn't. Jessica predicted that the guy traveled for work, but it looks like he may also have connections to hospitals. Every kidnapping victim has a relative who works for a hospital near the town where she was abducted."

"Brett is retired," she pointed out.

"Semiretired. He consults at Boston General and at Cape Cod General."

"I hadn't realized that."

"Two weeks before Everly was taken, Brett took the girls to a fund-raising event at the hospital here. There was face-painting. Food. Therapy dogs. They had a blast."

"And you think the kidnapper was there?"

"Not just me. The FBI special crimes unit has been investigating all the cases. After Brett mentioned the fund-raiser, we checked with the other families. Every one of them had brought the victim to an event at the hospital in the weeks prior to the kidnapping."

"So, maybe he doesn't have a job in medicine. Maybe, he's part of a fund-raising organization? Or, an event-planning company?"

"Good thoughts, and we're checking in to all those possibilities."

"This could be over soon."

"And when it is, you'll want my family to step out of your life?" he said, the comment so surprising, it almost didn't register.

"I never said that, Henry."

"So, it's just me you'll want to say goodbye to."

"I don't want to say goodbye to anyone. I want to get inside and get to work. It's going to take me longer than usual to get things ready for opening," she replied, climbing out of the SUV and closing the door. She ran to the diner and unlocked it, darting inside and shutting the door before she could change her mind, go back to the SUV and tell Henry that she would be happy if they never had to say goodbye. Not for any length of time.

She watched through a window as he drove away.

It was what she wanted. She should have been happy.

All she felt was tired.

Her cell phone rang as she trudged into the kitchen, and she thought it might be him. No one else called at odd hours of the day.

"Hello?" she said, holding the phone between her ear and her uninjured shoulder, expecting to hear Henry's voice.

"I know what you did," someone said, the tone raspy and harsh. Maybe male. Maybe female. It was impossible to distinguish.

"Who is this?" she demanded, and she was

surprised that her voice wasn't shaking. That she sounded confident rather than terrified.

"I know what you did," the person repeated.

The hair on her arms stood up, her stomach clenching with fear. "I haven't done anything."

The person chuckled. "You've done plenty. Eventually, you'll have to pay for it."

"Whoever you are, you've obviously got the wrong number." She hung up.

The phone rang again.

She answered, because she felt almost compelled to.

"Sometimes, it's good to mind your own business. Sometimes, doing anything else can get a woman in trouble," the person said.

"You have the wrong number," she said and hung up again.

The next time the phone rang, she ignored it, turning off the ringer so she wouldn't hear it as she set the dining-room tables.

Outside, the sun had just begun to rise and the street beyond the diner was dark. She could see shadows moving as the cold winter wind blew through pine-tree boughs.

Anyone could be hiding out there, watching her.

Her skin crawled, and she had the absurd urge to call Henry and tell her what had happened.

But what would she say? That someone had

made a prank call? That it had scared her because the caller had said he knew what she had done, and she had, in fact, done something. She'd stolen tens of thousands of dollars' worth of antique jewelry from her abusive ex, and she was terrified he was coming to seek revenge.

"It wasn't Patrick," she said, her words echoing hollowly in the empty dining room.

Someone knocked on the back door, and she jumped, her heart in her throat, her pulse racing.

It was locked.

Or, it should be.

She hadn't been to work in nearly a month. It was possible the night crew was getting lackadaisical. She doubted Ernie would allow it, but just in case, she grabbed a knife from the butcherblock on the counter as she walked across the dark kitchen and checked.

The doorknob wiggled as she approached.

She saw it clearly despite the darkness.

"Who's there?" she called.

No one answered, and the terror she'd been trying to hold at bay surged up. She hurried into the office—the only windowless space in the diner—and called 911.

Henry didn't have a problem taking no for an answer, and he certainly had no desire to push for a relationship that wasn't wanted by both parties.

In the years since Diane's death, he'd dated a few times. He'd found the experiences to be, for the most part, awkward and uncomfortable. If Tessa had been any of the women he'd gone out with, he'd have driven away and not given the relationship a second thought.

He didn't need to add people to his life.

It was filled by the twins and his work.

But somehow, Tessa had woven herself into the fabric of his family. He was never surprised when he arrived at his in-laws' for the weekend and found her there. Often, she'd be sitting at the kitchen table, snapping peas for Brett or singing 1950s tunes with Rachelle. Twice, he and the girls had arrived, and Tessa had been rubbing the wood banister with beeswax and listening to Rachelle tell stories about Diane.

Seeing her with his family had become the norm, and he didn't want that to change. He doubted she did, either. He'd watched her with the girls. He'd heard the laughter in her voice when she'd asked questions about their friends in Montessori school and heard stories about their mortal enemies. He'd seen it in her eyes as she'd listened to Everly describe the horrors of ballet class.

It was her gentleness with Aria that touched

him most. On two different Saturday evenings, Tessa had sat next to Aria and listened as she'd described her favorite books.

Her attention had never wavered.

She hadn't pulled out her phone or glanced at the clock.

She'd treated Aria as if she was the most important person she had ever met. She did the same with his in-laws and with Everly, giving each of them every bit of her attention when they were conversing. She never seemed to get tired of Everly's chatter or Rachelle's stories, or of Brett's description of his years working as the top neurosurgeon in Massachusetts.

He liked that about her.

He liked her.

The more time he spent with her, the deeper his admiration grew.

But she was hiding something.

He was as certain of that as he was that Everly would not be dancing in *Swan Lake* one day.

He pulled into the drive-thru of an all-night coffee shop and ordered two coffees. One with cream and sugar. One black and as strong as the barista could make it. It had been a week of twelve-hour days spent poring over the case files related to the serial kidnapper. Yesterday, he'd visited one of the two men who'd staged the altercation that had drawn Kayla away from

Tessa's hospital room. Unlike his buddies, he'd given a few indications that he might be willing to talk. Unfortunately, he didn't seem to know much. Just that his buddy Ezra Standard had been hitchhiking off the Cape and been picked up by a man who had offered him ten thousand dollars to off a lady at the hospital. The guy hadn't said why, and Ezra hadn't cared. He had an addiction that needed to be fed, and it took money to do that.

Yesterday's interview hadn't revealed anything, and Henry had returned to the field office exhausted and frustrated. He'd filed a report, done some overdue paperwork and finally arrived at the Cape four hours after the twins' bedtime. He hadn't missed the fatigue in Rachelle's eyes when he'd walked into the kitchen and seen her reading a magazine and sipping a cup of tea. She wasn't getting any younger, and he couldn't keep asking her to step in when he couldn't be there for the girls.

Returning to the diner, he frowned as he pulled up and parked in the alley beside it. A police car was parked at the curb. The place wouldn't open for another hour and the only reason he could think of for the cruiser to be there was if it had been called out.

He got out of the SUV and walked to the front door. He could see Tessa setting wrapped silverware on tables. Officer Kayla Delphina was sitting in a chair nearby, a small notebook in her hand and a frown on her face.

Whatever had happened, she wasn't happy about it.

He knocked on the door, and Tessa jumped, dropping the silverware she'd been placing and whirling to face the door.

When she saw him, she sagged in relief.

"It's unlocked," she called. "Come on in."

He stepped into the diner, a coffee cup in each hand. "What's going on?"

"Nothing serious," she replied.

"How about you let us be the judge of that?" Kayla responded.

"Good idea," Henry agreed. "What happened?"

"It was a prank phone call," Tessa said hurriedly. "I got spooked. That's all. Like I said, it was nothing."

"You said someone knocked on the back door," Kayla reminded her.

"Well, yes, but that could have been anyone."

"How often do people knock on the back door this time of morning?" Henry asked, handing her the coffee with cream and sugar and offering the other cup to Kayla.

"No, thanks. Chief has me on graveyard since I messed up at the hospital, and I'm so filled with caffeine, I may never sleep again. Henry's question is a legitimate one, Tess. Do you often get early morning visitors?"

"No," she admitted.

"Have you ever had an early morning visit right after receiving a prank call?" Kayla persisted, and Tessa frowned.

"This is the first time I've received a prank call," Tessa admitted.

"What did the caller say?" Henry asked, lifting the cell phone that was lying on a table nearby. It was hers. He recognized the case.

"Nothing that made any sense." She took a sip of coffee, her gaze on the phone.

"Can you be a little more specific?"

"He said he knew what I had done," she replied, the word rushing out, her gaze on the phone, the table, the floor, the wall. Anywhere but Henry.

"You're sure it was a man?" Kayla asked.

"No. It could have been a woman."

"But you said *he*," Henry pointed out.

"Unintentionally."

"Because there's someone you were thinking of? Someone who might want to scare you?"

"The kidnapper pops to mind," Kayla offered before Tessa could respond.

Too bad.

Henry would have liked to hear her answer.

He had a feeling the kidnapper hadn't been

the first person to pop into her mind. He'd noticed the scar on her face. He'd seen another on the inside of her forearm. Just a jagged pale line that looked like it had come from a broken glass. She'd told him very little about her past, but he knew she'd come from a tough neighborhood, that her mother had been a drug addict, that she'd made enough of her own mistakes as a teen and young adult to have a little more sympathy for the woman who'd raised her. She'd mentioned a relationship but hadn't gone into specifics.

That seemed to be Tessa's MO: very little information and very few details.

Which wasn't going to help her if she was hiding from something or someone from her past.

"Was that what you were thinking?" he asked. "That the kidnapper might have contacted you?"

"Not really, but it makes more sense than…"

"What?"

"Nothing." She set her coffee on the hostess station and grabbed more silverware.

"We can't help you if you don't tell us the truth," he said, exasperated, frustrated, worried.

He wanted to protect her.

She wasn't making it easy.

He was about to tell her that when something crashed through the window a few feet away, smashing the pane of glass and shattering it into millions of tiny shards.

"Get down!" he shouted, diving toward Tessa and tackling her to the ground as light flashed and a ball of fire shot across the room.

# SIX

The fire alarm screamed and smoke filled the air, but the fire seemed to be contained to a small area near the shattered window. Tessa noticed that at the same time she noticed a dark figure standing in the street. Tall and lean. A hat pulled over his eyes. She couldn't make out the details through the haze of smoke, but she was certain Henry and Kayla saw him, too. Kayla was calling into her radio, asking for backup. Henry was lying still, pressing her into the floor with his weight.

"I need to get a fire extinguisher," she gasped, shoving against his firm chest. "There's one behind the hostess station."

He didn't move, and she couldn't move him. He was at least five inches taller and probably sixty pounds heavier.

"Henry! I can't let this place go up in flames. It's all Ernie and Betty have!" she nearly shouted.

He finally shifted his weight, grabbing her

hand and dragging her to the hostess station, his focus on the street. The man was gone, but he'd looked a lot like the kidnapper. The same build and height, anyway. She knew that. Would have said it, but Henry dragged the extinguisher and sprayed it at the fire.

"Wait here," he ordered as he strode toward the foam-covered debris that was in the middle of the shattered glass.

She followed, because she wasn't about to let him face danger while she cowered near the wall.

He toed the mess, glanced at Kayla. "It's out, but the fire department should still respond. I'm not sure if any damage has been done to the floor."

"The place is built on a cement slab. No one is going to fall through if it has," Tessa replied, her stomach churning as she stared at the gray-black foam and broken glass.

"We still have to have the fire marshal clear it," Kayla explained, the screaming fire alarm nearly drowning her words. Like Henry, she was staring into the street, eyeing the area where the man had been standing.

"He was the same height and build as the kidnapper," Tessa offered, and Henry tensed.

"Stay with Tessa," he shouted above the racket and stepped toward the shattered window.

"Maybe you should wait for backup to arrive before you go out there," Tessa cautioned, grabbing the back of his coat and trying to stop his momentum.

"Tess," he said, meeting her eyes as he gently extracted her hands. "I do this for a living. I'll be fine."

"But—"

"I'll be fine," he repeated, kissing her forehead like she'd seen him do dozens of times with the twins. Only she wasn't one of the twins, and the kiss didn't feel at all paternal. It felt like a promise that things would be okay and like a glimpse of things to come.

Things she'd once dreamed of but had given up on long ago. Love. Commitment. Happily-ever-after. The cute house. The white picket fence. The kids and dogs and forever.

She didn't dare let herself dream again.

She'd told herself that dozens of times in the past few weeks, but her fickle heart still seemed determined to do it.

Henry was gone before she could tell him any of those things.

Not that she would have.

She'd have stood mute. Just like she was now. The alarm screaming, smoke swirling, the wreckage of the diner sprawled in front of her.

"Can you cut the alarm?" Kayla yelled.

She nodded, rushing to the kitchen and the panel that controlled the system. She shut it off, her ears ringing in the sudden silence.

"That's better," Kayla murmured, crouching next to the broken glass. "Now I can think, and what I'm thinking is that things have gotten interesting."

"I'm not sure I'd call this mess interesting."

"I'm talking about you and Henry."

"There is no me and Henry."

"Right. Because you're off relationships for the rest of your life."

"I think we have more important things to think about," Tessa replied, sidestepping the conversation. Because Henry had been right. She was good at it.

"I'm not thinking about it. I'm commenting on it. What I'm thinking about is the fact that someone threw a Molotov cocktail through the window. A brick was attached to the bottle." She gestured to a red brick nearly covered with foam. "I guess he wanted to make certain it went through the glass."

"I guess so," Tessa responded, staring out the window, watching the alley Henry had disappeared into. Sure, he did this for a living, but that didn't mean it wasn't dangerous. It didn't mean things couldn't go wrong.

"There's no guessing involved in police work.

It's about facts and evidence. The fact is, he tossed the bottle attached to the brick. I can see the duct tape here." She pointed.

Tessa glanced at the mess. "I can see it, too."

"What I can't see is a motive. It certainly wasn't attempted murder. It would take a lot more power than that makeshift bomb has to bring this place down," Kayla continued.

"I'm assuming someone wanted to scare me."

"Who and why?"

"I have no idea."

"There seem to be a lot of things you don't have any idea about," Kayla said.

Tessa met her eyes. "If you're implying something, just come out and say it instead."

"I'm not implying anything. I'm stating another fact. Someone was here this morning. Trying to scare you. Trying to accomplish something else. I don't know, and you don't seem willing to provide any information."

"I've provided as much as I have." That wasn't the truth. Not all of it. She wanted to say more. She wanted to admit to her secrets, clear the air, stop hiding things that might hurt her, but silence was a hard thing to break. And she'd been silent for a long time.

Nine years with Patrick.

Three years without.

The words wouldn't come. No matter how much she knew they probably should.

A police car pulled into view and parked at the curb in front of the building. Chief Simpson stepped out. He strode toward the building, his expression grim and hard in the grayish morning light.

"Is the fire contained?" he asked as he stepped through the shattered window.

"Yes," Kayla responded.

"Good." He took out a camera and started taking photos of the brick, the broken glass and several charred rags that were visible beneath the foam. "Was anyone else here when this happened?"

"Special Agent Miller. He's gone after a man we think is the perpetrator."

"You should have called that in, Officer. He may need backup." He spoke into his radio, issuing commands.

The diner was a mess, the air heavy with smoke, the ceiling near the window stained with soot. The five-foot-tall window that looked out onto Commercial Street had been demolished.

How much time would it take to clean the place up and replace the window?

How long would Ernie's have to be closed? Days? Weeks?

How many employees would be late paying

bills because of the fire? How many of them would suffer because of this?

"How about we open the back door?" the chief suggested. "Try to get some of this smoke out of here."

Tessa ran to do as he'd asked, shoving open the door and letting cold winter air blow in. The cross ventilation seemed to work, as the haziness in the kitchen started to dissipate.

Voices drifted in from the service area, and she assumed other officers had arrived. She braced herself for the questions she knew would come. Who? Why?

She'd have to explain the prank call again.

She'd have to talk about the knock on the back door.

She'd have to convince herself that everything that had happened had everything to do with the kidnapper who was still on the loose.

And maybe it did.

*Probably* it did.

She had no reason to believe Patrick had found her.

She had no reason to think that he'd have bothered traveling across the country to taunt and terrify her.

If he'd been interested in finding her, she was sure that he could have done it years ago. She'd purchased a new identity, but she hadn't tried terribly hard to cover her tracks. She'd been too scared and too desperate to do much more than plan her escape and follow through on it. She had only used cash, of course. She'd pawned her jewelry in shops far away from California. But she'd also bought an old car off a lot close to the mall where she'd parked the one he'd given her.

If Patrick had wanted to, he could have asked around and figured that out. He could have learned her new name. He could have searched databases, and eventually, he might have been able to track her down. He hadn't. He'd started dating Sheila, his partner Ryan's widow. He'd married her.

He had a new life with a new woman, and according to the society section of the *Napa Valley Times*, he was living the same life of refined wealth as he always had.

He hadn't found Tessa, because he hadn't wanted to.

She'd been telling herself that for three years.

She'd almost convinced herself it was true.

She hoped it was, because she'd come a long way to become the person her grandmother had wanted her to be. She'd traveled thousands of miles. She'd taken hundreds of hours of classes at the community college. She'd worked nearly every day from the time she'd been given a chance at the diner until she'd been injured at the hospital.

She was close to achieving her goals.

She didn't want to have to leave town and give up all of that.

But lately, there had been a lot of whispering around town. She had heard the murmured conversations when she had attended church. She had noticed that people had stopped talking when she had walked into doctors' offices. She understood that she had become a curiosity— that woman who had arrived in town one day without much of a story. The one who'd stopped a kidnapping. Who had been nearly murdered.

The fire at the diner would bring more whispering and more curiosity.

"Tessa, is everything okay back there?" Kayla called.

"Yes," she replied as she hurried back into the service area.

It looked just as terrible as it had when she'd walked into the kitchen, the air a little clearer, but the soot and smoke-stained dining area even more noticeable. She reached for the pile of burned rags that sat on the floor near the brick and broken glass, anxious to put some order to the chaos and clear some of the mess.

"Don't touch anything," Kayla barked, and Tessa jerked her hand back.

"Sorry."

"It's okay." Kayla glanced out the window. The chief was standing near his cruiser, talking to the fire marshal. "I'm just already in the hot seat because of the incident at the hospital." Her cheeks flushed with embarrassment. "If I mess this up, the chief will fire me."

"I doubt that. You're good at your job, and he knows it."

"He's my uncle. He doesn't know anything except that he feels obligated and that he couldn't deny the strength of my application or my experience."

"Your uncle?" That was something she hadn't been aware of. In a town where everyone talked about everyone, she was surprised she hadn't heard about the family connection.

"It's not common knowledge, but yes."

"Is there a reason why it isn't?"

"Like you, I try to keep my story to myself."

"I'm not keeping anything to myself."

"No? Then why doesn't anyone know anything about you? Where you came from? Why you arrived in Provincetown one summer and stayed?"

"I'm from California," she offered.

"That doesn't tell me much of anything. Here's what I do know. People don't just decide and make homes on the cold beaches of Provincetown. Me? I came because my mother told me stories of meeting my father here. I came out of curiosity the year I turned eighteen. Eventually, I decided it would be a nice place to settle."

"Your father must be happy to have you here."

"I haven't seen my father since I was six. He couldn't care less where I am, and the feeling is mutual. I didn't bother mentioning him or my relationship to him when I applied to work for the police department the first time."

"The first time?"

"I applied three years in a row. The first year, the chief called me out. He'd done a background check, and he knew who my father was. He told me to go back to Boston and get a job there because he couldn't have his town claiming nepotism. I applied the next year and the next."

"You're persistent."

"I wanted the job. I like Provincetown. It felt like home the first day I visited, and it hasn't stopped feeling that way. My third time applying, the chief must have decided I'd earned my stripes as a beat cop in Boston. He hired me, and here I am. Walking a thin line between having a job and not. So, if you're keeping information from us, now would be a good time to tell me," she said.

Tessa wanted to speak into the sudden silence. She wanted to voice the truth, but—just like always—the words were stuck in her throat and refused to be released.

Outside, an old Chevy truck bounced over the curb behind the chief's cruiser. Tessa recognized the glossy blue paint and the shiny chrome rims. Ernie loved the truck. He wouldn't love what had happened to the diner.

He jumped out, racing toward the broken window, Betty just a few steps behind him.

"It's true!" he cried as he walked through the opening. "A bomb went off!"

He looked around wildly, spotted Tessa and strode toward her.

"Ernie, I'm so sor—" she began.

He dragged her into his arms, wrapping her in a bear hug that threatened to crack her ribs. "You're okay!"

"Of course I am," she mumbled against his scratchy flannel shirt. It smelled like pipe tobacco and peppermint, and she imagined that if she'd ever had a grandfather, his hugs would have smelled exactly like that.

"You're sure?" He backed up, his hands wrapped around her biceps.

"I'm fine. But, the diner—"

"Honey, the diner can be fixed."

"The window—"

"Can be replaced. People can't. Betty and I were eating breakfast when we heard about the explosion on the police scanner. All I could think about was you." He stepped back, pulling a handkerchief from his pocket and wiping his forehead with it. "I haven't run that fast since I thought Danny Erickson was going to ask Betty to the seventh-grade dance before I had a chance to."

"You ran pretty fast the other day when you thought Kendal Jameson was going to let her kids grab the last few pieces of apple pie at the church social," Betty said as she hurried up behind him. "I'm so glad you're okay, Tessa. We were worried sick. We tried to call the chief to ask if there'd been injuries, but he wasn't answering his phone." She eyed the shattered diner window, the soot-stained ceiling and smoke-marred interior. "Well, isn't this a pretty sight."

"Pretty! It's going to cost a fortune to replace the window and get the smoke out of the walls and off the tables," Ernie grumbled, obviously back to his normal taciturn nature.

"Insurance will cover it, and we'll get a nice new, double-paned window out of the deal. I'm not going to say I'm sorry about it. This place costs a fortune to heat in the winter. Plus, we'll get some new flooring—"

"New flooring! There's just a tiny black spot on the old one," Ernie protested.

"Tiny? It's at least two feet of singed tiles.

Which doesn't make me sad. I never did like this floor," Betty commented.

"What's wrong with the floor?" Ernie demanded.

"It's covering beautiful wood."

"Nicked wood that needed to be refinished. Putting tile over it was cheaper than paying someone to do that."

"We were broke when we bought this place. We barely scraped together enough money for the down payment. It's nearly forty years later. The mortgage has been paid off for twenty years We're not broke, and I'd like to update the place. Now is the perfect time to do it," Betty said cheerfully.

"Update what? This place is timeless," Ernie responded.

"You always say that, but I'm certain Tessa would agree—"

The sound of a ringing phone stopped their conversation, Tessa hurried to the old-fashioned rotary phone that hung on the wall near the hostess station.

"The place is closed. It's a crime scene," Kayla reminded her, as if the diner would have opened on time windowless and soot-stained and smelling like fire-extinguisher chemicals.

She nodded as she grabbed the receiver.

"Ernie's Diner. I'm sorry, but we can't take any reservations today."

"I don't want reservations," the same raspy-voiced person who'd called her cell phone said. "I want to know how scared you felt when those flames shot through the diner."

"Who is this?" she demanded.

She must have shouted the question, because Kayla was suddenly beside her, pressing in close and trying to hear the conversation.

Tessa shifted the phone, the taunting words seeping into the room. "It doesn't matter."

Kayla nudged her and whispered, "Keep him talking," while she ran outside and grabbed the chief's arm.

Hopefully, she was trying to get a trace on the call.

"It matters to me," she said.

"It didn't matter three years ago, did it?"

She went cold with fear, her pulse sloshing in her ears. "Patrick?"

A quiet click was the only answer.

Kayla had returned, and she scowled. "Did he hang up?"

"Yes," she said, surprised she could speak past her terror.

"Who is Patrick?"

She'd obviously heard Tessa say the name.

Denying the relationship would be foolish. "An old boyfriend."

"Is there some reason why he'd be calling you here?"

"I…'m not sure."

"But you think that was him on the phone?" Kayla pressed.

"I don't know if it was him."

"Then, why did you say his name?"

"He mentioned something about three years ago. That's when we broke up."

"And, when you arrived here," Kayla pointed out.

"Yes."

"Does he know you work here?"

"As far as I know, he doesn't even know I'm in Provincetown."

"Does anyone in town know about him?"

"No. Why?"

"The guys who were hired to pull off the hit at the hospital are locals. Their families have lived in this town for generations."

"I hadn't realized that."

"Why would you have? They don't make a habit of eating breakfast at family establishments like this one. Plus, they're in and out of town, in and out of trouble and in and out of jail so much we almost never see them." Kayla shrugged. "I thought maybe one of them knew about your ex and gave the information to the kidnapper. But, maybe the kidnapper figured it out on his own. The internet makes it easy to find information about people."

"Why would he want information about my past?"

"Maybe he wanted to use it to get under your skin? To keep you off balance? Maybe to send you running? Because, if you run, you can't testify once he's caught?"

"Maybe." And, maybe Kayla was right. Maybe the kidnapper had figured out who she was, dug up information about Patrick and made the phone call.

Maybe.

But, Tessa knew she'd never mentioned Patrick to anyone. She hadn't kept any written record of their relationship. Even if someone had dug into her background, nothing about Patrick would have popped up, because she'd lived under a different name and had a different identity when she'd been with him.

Knowing that scared her.

If the information about the relationship was as difficult to find as she thought it would be, how had the kidnapper obtained it.

And, if he hadn't?

Who had made the call?

Patrick?

The thought filled her with cold fear.

She almost told Kayla her concern. She almost told her everything. It would have been a relief to get it out in the open, to tell the truth and see what happened. But, the chief reentered the diner, the fire marshal beside him, and the opportunity was lost in the volley of questions that were lobbed her way.

Henry chased the perp through the business district and into a more residential section of town. The guy was skinny and quick, hopping over fences and scrambling around cars, darting behind anything that he could find and ignoring Henry's demands that he stop.

That was fine.

Henry could run, too. He'd raced cross country in college, and he'd continued to run after he'd become an FBI agent. It kept him in shape and cleared his head.

He sprinted around a small boat parked in someone's driveway and followed the perp into a copse of trees. The sun had risen behind thick clouds, and the air was heavy with moisture.

He felt the first drop of rain as he clambered over a fallen log. Another drop splattered on his cheek. Up ahead, the perp was crashing through brambles, obviously not making any effort to be quiet. He was probably trying to reach the road.

Maybe he had a ride waiting. If so, he and the driver would both be under arrest. Henry had already called in their coordinates and the direction they were heading. He had no doubt the chief would have officers lining the road, waiting for the perp to appear.

Maybe the guy realized the road wasn't the smartest option. He veered south, his pace flagging, his energy obviously waning. He was slowing.

Henry had no intention of doing the same.

He could see the guy's dark clothes through the winter-sparse trees. He called out one last time, and then he sprang forward, tackling the guy and pinning him to the ground. He yanked a skinny arm up behind a scrawny back and realized the person he'd been chasing was a kid. Sixteen or seventeen, with a gangly body and a baby-smooth face. Not someone from the mid-twenties to early forties, as Henry had been expecting. Certainly not anyone who fit the criminal profile of the kidnapper. This kid looked terrified, his dark eyes rimmed with fatigue and filled with fear.

"Do you have any weapons on you?" Henry asked, easing up just enough so the kid could breathe.

"No. My dad tried to give me a gun, but I told him I wasn't bringing it," the teen said. Not a hint of rebellion in his voice. If anything, he seemed subdued. Even, Henry thought, a little relieved.

"Your dad?" Henry patted worn jeans and a hole-filled jacket. No sign of a weapon. No wallet. No ID.

"Yes."

"What you're telling me is that your father asked you to bring a gun to town and blow up a restaurant?"

"Yes," the young man repeated.

"Where is your father?"

"I don't know. He drove me to the diner and said he'd park at the end of the street and wait until I…finished, but he drove away as soon as I did."

"Your father orchestrated this?" Henry asked, because he couldn't wrap his mind around the fact that this quiet, scrawny teenager had been pulled into a crime by the man who was supposed to be raising him.

"Yes."

It was one of the most bizarre stories Henry had ever heard, and he'd heard a lot of them. For some reason, coming from the teen's mouth, it sounded like the truth.

Henry pulled him to his feet. "What's your name?"

"Saige Banning."

"Your age?"

"Fifteen."

"You live around here?" he asked as he forced the boy to start walking toward the road.

"I'm from Wareham."

"That's two hours away. Not an easy commute for someone who can't drive."

"I have my learner's permit, and I told you, my dad drove me here."

"That's a difficult story to believe."

"Because, you don't know my father," Saige muttered, not trying to fight the forward momentum, not asking who Henry was, not demanding identification or protesting his capture.

Relieved.

That was the word Henry would put to Saige's expression.

"What's your father's name?"

"Tom."

"Same surname?"

"Unfortunately."

"You sound angry," Henry commented. Police lights flashed through the trees, and a car door slammed. Backup had finally arrived.

"My dad drove me out here to commit a crime. Then, he left me to face the consequences. So, yeah. I'm a little angry."

"Did your father tell you why he wanted you to commit the crime?"

"Money. That's all my father ever cares about."

"Apparently, you care about it, too. You agreed to do what he asked."

"My mother is sick. Her medicine costs four hundred bucks a month. My dad blows most of our cash on beer, and my mom spends what's left on food and school stuff for me. I finally got a job to try to help, but it doesn't pay enough to fill the prescription every month. My father said if we did this job, he'd give me enough money to cover the cost for six months."

"That was very generous of him," Henry said wryly.

Saige shrugged "He probably wasn't going to give me anything, but I was desperate enough to take the chance. If Mom's kidney gets worse, she'll have to go on dialysis. We can't afford that, either. Not that it's going to matter. When she finds out what I did, it'll kill her." His voice broke, and Henry felt a sudden pang of sympathy. He didn't usually have compassion for people who committed crimes, but this kid was probably the least aggressive and most pitiful criminal he'd ever set eyes on.

"She'll weather the storm, Saige, that's what parents do," he said.

"Maybe, but I feel like she's already had to weather too much." Saige stumbled.

"Careful," Henry said.

The teen nodded mutely, and Henry realized he was crying, tears streaming down his cheeks and probably blinding him.

"Look…" he began, intending to offer words of comfort, maybe a little hope that things weren't as bad as they seemed.

A branch cracked behind him, and the hair on his nape stood on end.

He leaped to the left, pulling Saige with him as gunfire exploded behind them. A bullet glanced off his arm, breaking his grip on the teen as they fell to the ground.

"Get up and run, Saige!" someone shouted, as a barrage of bullets hit the ground a few feet away. "Move it, kid!"

To Henry's surprise, Saige stayed where he was, lying inches away, his hands pressed into dead leaves and dry earth. He had dark eyes, dark hair that fell straight to his shoulders and a look of complete shock on his face.

He wasn't the kind of hardened criminal Henry usually dealt with, and he certainly didn't seem intent on escape. Despite the continued shouts from whoever had ambushed them, he stayed where he was, staring almost desperately into Henry's face.

"That's him. My father," he said as if he needed to explain the situation.

"I figured as much."

"I didn't know he was going to do this. I just thought we were trying to scare someone."

"It's okay."

"It's not okay," Saige said, his voice cracking. "You're bleeding."

Several police officers were shouting for the gunman to surrender, but the shooting had already stopped, the crash of footsteps through dry foliage signaling his retreat.

"I'll be fine. I want you to stay here and stay down. Okay? Don't move. The police don't know who you are. They don't know if you're armed. They might shoot if you suddenly pop up."

"What are you going to do?" Saige asked as Henry pulled his firearm from its holster.

"I'm going to make sure I don't get shot again," he responded. "Stay down," he warned one last time, and then he took off after the fleeing gunman.

He caught him on an unpaved road less than a quarter mile away. As scrawny as his son but not nearly as cooperative, he dropped his weapon as soon as Henry called for him to do so, and then tried to pull another.

"I wouldn't," Henry growled, his gun aimed straight at the man's gaunt face. Saige had said his father spent the family money on alcohol. It looked more like he spent it on methamphetamine.

"I'm not doing nothing," the man responded, his bald head beaded with sweat despite the frigid temperatures.

"Down on the ground. Spread eagle. Hands where I can see them," Henry ordered. "I'm sure you know the drill."

"You have no right to detain me. I'm just minding my own business, hunting."

"On Cape Cod?" Henry asked as the man dropped to his belly, his arms stretched to either side.

"No one told me I couldn't."

"You might want to think up a better story than that, Mr. Banning."

"How'd you know my name? That boy has been squealing, hasn't he? Singing a sad little song to the police to keep himself out of trouble. Well let me tell you, copper—"

"Special Agent Henry Miller. I'm with the Federal Bureau of Investigation," Henry interrupted.

"The FBI?"

"Yes." Henry found a Glock pistol in the man's waistband and a knife tucked in his sock.

"Anything else I should know about?" he asked as he removed the man's wallet and cuffed his hands behind his back.

"You're with the FBI?" he repeated.

Henry nodded as he scanned the driver's license. Tom Banning. Thirty-five. From Wareham. So far, Saige's story checked out. "So, are you ready to change your story, Tom?" he asked. "Because I have a feeling that when we run your ID through the system, we might just find some warrants."

"I've got no warrants. I keep myself out of trouble."

"Is that what you call this?" Henry asked, hefting him to his feet a lot less gently than he had Saige.

"I call this a job, and it was supposed to be an easy one. A thousand bucks to cause a little chaos at that diner. No one was supposed to get hurt, and no one did. Am I right?"

"I'm bleeding, so I'd say someone did."

"That was an accident. I was aiming for the ground."

"Who is paying you?"

"Don't know. Don't care."

"Someone contacted you. Give me a name. Maybe we can work something out that doesn't involve you spending the rest of your life in jail for shooting a federal agent."

"I wasn't trying to shoot you, man!" Tom protested. "I was trying to cause a distraction, so that my wimpy son could escape."

"Then you're a pretty bad shot, because you

did manage to shoot me, and that could be construed as attempted murder."

"Murder! I didn't do no such thing! I didn't even toss the cocktail in the diner. The boy did. He's a minor, and you can't do a thing to him."

"Sure we can, and we can do more to you, so how about you tell me who hired you?"

"I already told you, I don't know."

"You may not have a name, but you saw a face."

"Maybe I did, but he's no one I know. No one from around here. Looked too ritzy to be from my neck of the woods and too highbrow to be from Provincetown."

"That's not a lot of information."

"It's all I have."

"Where'd you meet?"

"At Sally's Bar. Right off Route Six. It's my favorite drinking hole."

"When was that?"

"Two nights ago. Said he needed a job done. Asked if I wanted some work. He was buying the shots, so I said sure. He gave me two hundred up front."

"When is he supposed to give you the rest?"

"Tonight. I took a couple of pictures on my phone and I sent them to him. Once he sees them, he'll pay."

"You're planning to meet up with him again?"

"Nah. He's transferring the money straight into my account. Did it with the first two-hundred. Shouldn't be a problem to do it again. Once it's there, I'm buying myself a steak dinner."

"That would be a great plan, but you forgot something," Henry said, hoping that the bank transfer or phone number could be traced to the perp.

"What?"

"You're going to be spending tonight, and every other night for a very long time, in jail."

"Hey! I told you what I know. You owe me."

"You shot me, Tom. That's not something I take lightly. But if you can pick your friend out of a lineup, I might not press charges."

"A lineup? Sure. I can do that. You show me some pictures. I'll tell you which guy paid me. Then we'll be square, right?"

"That's up to the chief of police to decide. For right now, how about I read you your rights?"

"Man! This was supposed to be any easy thousand!" Tom protested.

Henry ignored him as he read Tom his Miranda rights and marched him back in the direction they'd come.

# SEVEN

It was well past sunset when Tessa was finally allowed to return home. She'd spent most of the day at the police station, answering endless questions.

What had she seen?

What did she know?

Who would want to hurt her? Damage the diner? Cause trouble?

She'd mentioned the kidnapper a dozen times. She'd mentioned Patrick once or twice. She'd given his name to Chief Simpson, providing as little background on their relationship as she could get away with.

She hadn't revealed that they'd lived together for nine years, that they'd met when she was eighteen, that Patrick had told her everything she'd wanted to hear, and that she'd believed him because she was young and desperate to be loved.

She hadn't told him about the first thrown

vase or the second one or any of the ones that had followed. She hadn't mentioned the bruises, the sprained wrists, the cracked ribs, the turtle-neck sweaters that hid the fingerprints on her neck.

She hadn't told him about the stolen antique jewelry that was locked in a safe-deposit box at Provincetown Savings and Loan. She hadn't told him about the purchased identity or the changed name.

She hadn't told him who she really was.

Even if she'd wanted to, she wasn't sure she could have.

Her hands were shaking as she unlocked the cottage door, but she pasted on a smile as she turned to wave at Kayla, who had driven her home. She got a quick wave in return, and then she was alone, standing on the threshold, terrified to step inside.

What if he was there, waiting in the shadows for her return?

What if she walked into the living room, and he was stretched out on the couch, a glass of wine in his hand and a look of hatred in his eyes.

Would she have time to call the police?

Would she be fast enough to run away?

"Stop it!" she hissed, stepping into the house and locking the door. She hung her purse on the hook near the door, shrugged out of her coat and put it in the closet.

The chief had had patrols cars riding by the house all day. He'd assured her that no one had been near the place.

He'd also told her that the person who'd tossed the Molotov cocktail had been apprehended, and that he was being interviewed.

She'd asked about Henry, and she'd received no response.

She'd asked again, and she'd been told he was at the medical center. When she'd asked why, the chief had explained that he'd received a minor injury while chasing down a suspect.

She'd called and texted Henry several times, and when he hadn't responded, she'd finally given up.

Being with Patrick had taught her not to chase things that weren't meant to be.

She shuddered, hurrying to the front windows to close the curtains. To her surprise, one of the windows was unlocked. She hadn't left it that way.

Had she?

The past few weeks had been hectic. She'd been off her schedule, running to appointments and trying to keep up with her studies. There may have been a day or two when she'd opened the window to let salty winter air sweep away the musty scent of the locked-up house.

Had she forgotten to lock it?

That didn't seem like something she'd do.

She was a creature of habit and almost obsessive about her need to make certain the doors and windows were shut and locked.

She'd been afraid for years.

Being shot hadn't improved on that.

She crept through the living room and walked into the tiny dining room. A square space with built-in corner hutches, it contained a small table, a chair and her laptop. A pile of books sat beside the computer, and the pad of paper and pen she used for notetaking was on top of the stack.

She'd thought she'd left it next to her bed, but she'd been forgetful lately, misplacing her keys and her phone more times than she cared to admit.

She liked to see her life as a dance she choreographed, each step carefully planned and executed. Lately, her perfect waltz seemed more like a fumbling square dance.

She walked down the hall and into the only bedroom, hesitating in the doorway for a moment before stepping into the room. Usually, she closed the door before she left the house for the day. Today, the door had been left open. She flicked on the light, her heart racing as she surveyed the interior. There was no bed skirt, and she could see beneath the full bed frame. There was nothing there that shouldn't be. Just a few storage boxes pushed up against the wall. Not big enough for anyone to hide behind.

The closet door was open, too, her work pants and shirts hanging neatly next to a few church dresses.

She crossed the room, pulled out the bottom drawer of her dresser and lifted out the file folder that contained her rental agreement and her banking information. It didn't look like it had been touched. All her clothes were still neatly folded and tucked into the other drawers. Her pillows were sitting in the same positions she'd left them.

Nothing was out of place, and yet, she felt as if everything were.

"You are being paranoid," she said, speaking the words out loud, as if that would make them true.

She walked into the bathroom and pulled back the shower curtain. Nothing there. The soaps and shampoo were still sitting in the shower caddy. The towels were neatly folded on the shelves above the toilet. It was a small bathroom with a tiny window that a child could probably fit through.

Tessa hadn't bothered to see if she could, but she didn't think a grown man could squeeze his shoulders through the narrow space. She made certain it was locked and walked to the kitchen, eyeing the scrubbed-out sink and the window that looked out over the postage-stamp-size backyard.

Everything looked exactly the way she'd left it.

She checked the lock on the window and walked into the mudroom. The laundry detergent, bucket and mop were sitting in front of the bolted back door. She'd left them there on purpose—a makeshift alarm system until she could talk Ernie in to having one installed.

There was only one space left in the house.

The basement. She'd asked Ernie's permission to put a bolt on the interior door when she'd moved in. He'd laughed but told her to knock herself out.

She eyed the bolt. It was locked, the heavy Scottie-dog-shaped doorstop sitting to the right of the door frame.

Which made no sense, because the door opened in that direction.

She frowned, moving the dog back into place on the left side of the door. She had to have moved it. There was no one in the house, and there was no way anyone could have walked down into the basement and bolted themselves in. She knew that. She also knew there was no way she was going to sleep without checking, to be certain.

She slid the bolt free and turned the old-fashioned skeleton key that she kept in the lock. The door swung open on well-oiled hinges, and she reached for the cord that hung from the ceiling. She tugged it and light spilled down the wooden stairs.

The floor of the basement was packed clay, as the house had been built in the days of root-cellar storage. It smelled musty and damp, and she almost decided to trust that it was empty, close the door and lock it again.

"If you don't do it now, you're going to have to do it later. Just get it over with," she muttered, descending the first few steps and pausing near the old verse etched into a wooden beam near the stairs: Joshua 1:9.

She had no idea who had left it there. When she'd first seen it, she hadn't even been certain that Joshua was a book of the Bible. That embarrassed her now, but it was the truth. She'd figured it out when she'd Googled and found words that seemed to have been written directly to her:

*Have I not commanded you? Be strong and courageous. Do not be afraid. Do not be dis-*

*couraged. For the Lord your God will be with you wherever you go.*

It had seemed an odd coincidence that a fear-filled broken woman would rent a house with that verse written in it, and Tessa hadn't been able to stop thinking about it. Eventually, she'd decided to attend church for the first time since her grandmother's death.

She'd felt like the woman with the scarlet letter sewn to her dress, but she'd put on the most conservative outfit she'd owned and headed into the least intimidating church she could find. No fancy bell tower or stained-glass windows. Just a white building with clapboard siding and a gravel parking lot. Faith Community Church had welcomed her with open arms. No one had commented on the fact that her ears were pierced five times each or that she'd been too uncomfortable to sing the hymns. She'd returned the next week, and then the next.

She'd found sanctuary on the hard wooden pew, and she had found her faith in the old leather Bible that Betty had lent her.

So, why was she standing on the basement stairs afraid of what might be lurking in the musty space below?

God was in control.

She knew that.

She could walk down the last few steps into the basement with confidence.

She *would* walk down them with confidence.

One. Two. Three. Four. Five.

She reached the bottom and tugged the cord that hung from the ceiling. Nothing. The bulb must have blown out. She headed back upstairs, determined to find a bulb and search the cellar.

She was halfway up when the door slammed shut and the bolt slid home, metal scraping against metal just like it always did.

Shocked, she raced to the landing and turned the doorknob. Locked. She almost banged on the door. She almost asked who was there, but she was terrified that whoever it was would open the door and show himself. Patrick? Everly's kidnapper?

She didn't want to face either of them.

Not alone and unarmed.

Not ever.

She backed away. One careful step down at a time.

"Is it dark enough for you?" a man called.

She didn't respond.

Seconds later, the light above the stairs went out and the house went completely silent. He'd cut off the power, and the electric furnace had stopped its quiet humming.

The boards above her creaked, and something

slid across the floor. The dining room table? The couch? One of the boxes she'd stored under her bed?

Whatever he was doing, it was buying her time.

The basement had an exterior door. An old-fashioned hatch-style that was at an angle to the ground. Five steps led from it to the basement floor.

All she had to do was figure out a way to open it, and she'd be home-free.

She felt her way across the inky blackness, guessing at the placement of the door. She hadn't been in the basement too often. She stored Christmas decorations in boxes on shelves that had been drilled into the limestone wall. There were garden tools hanging from hooks, and she sometimes used them.

Mostly, though, she avoided the cold, dank space.

Now, she wished she'd paid more attention to what it contained.

The sound of her cell phone ringing carried through the darkness. Henry finally returning her messages?

If it was him, would he worry if she didn't answer?

Would he come looking for her?

The ringing stopped, and she thought she

heard someone humming. The sound shivered along her spine as she finally found the stairs that led to the exterior door. She expected resistance when she pushed it. To her surprise, it began opening immediately. No lock held it in place. No rusty hinges caught as she pushed. She waited, afraid that the intruder would see her emerging from the basement and chase her down.

The basement door was at the back of the house, beside the entrance to the mudroom. She could see it from the window of her bedroom, but she'd left the curtains closed.

Was he in there? If so, she could easily escape without being seen.

If he was in the kitchen or dining room, he could look out and see the open cellar door.

The floorboards creaked and something else slid across the floor.

He was moving boxes. He had to be. Which meant he was in her room. The curtains *were* closed, and he wouldn't have opened them.

Now or never.

She eased the basement door open, cold rain splattering her face as she crept up the stairs and closed the doors again. She raced across the yard, running toward the path that led to the beach. When she reached it, she glanced back, saw the beam of a flashlight dancing behind the curtains in her room.

She felt sick with fear, terrified that whoever was holding the light would open the curtains and realize she'd escaped. The light disappeared, and the back door flew open, a dark figure barreling outside.

Bigger than Patrick. Broader.

He hadn't seen her, and she wasn't going to give him an opportunity to. She took off, sprinting across the sand, rain dripping down her cheeks like icy tears.

Henry held the phone to his ear, listening as it went straight to voice mail. He left a message. His second one. "Tessa, it's Henry. Sorry it took so long to get back to you. I was dealing with a few problems. Give me a call when you have time."

"Are you going to wait a full fifteen minutes to make the next call, or just do it right now?" Saige asked, his scrawny arms wrapped around his legs as he sat on the floor near the fireplace.

*He* was one of the problems Henry had been dealing with.

Chief Simpson had wanted him to spend a night in the county jail. To teach him a lesson. The county prosecutor had been agreeable. Henry had spent several hours convincing them there were other choices. That had required calling the field office and asking Wren to intervene.

She and Jessica had made the drive from Boston to Wareham, picked up Saige's mother and transported her to Provincetown. Nancy Banning was as frail and weak as her son had made her sound, her face gaunt, her eyes sunken. She'd pled her case in Chief Simpson's small office, showing proof of her illness, of her son's three jobs and the money he'd spent on her medication. She'd tossed Saige's straight-A report cards on the chief's desk, and she'd cried.

In the end, the chief and prosecuting attorney hadn't stood a chance. They'd agreed to remand Saige to her custody on the condition that her husband not be allowed back in the house if he was released from county prison.

The likelihood of that happening was slim.

Tom had clammed up once he'd reached the precinct. Sobered up was more like it. He'd reeked of alcohol, the stench of it filling the patrol car he'd been transported in. He'd demanded an attorney, refusing to look at any mug shots or lineups until he had one present. The chief had called the county and asked for a public defender. Hopefully, they'd have one by the morning.

Not that it would make much of a difference.

Until they had more information from the
DNA hit, they had no list of suspects and no
photos to put in the lineup. Jessica seemed to
think they were getting close. She'd extracted
names and birthdates from a public family tree
posted online. Zebedee Cantor had been the
family member who'd collected the family history, matched DNA and entered the information. He was also the distant-relative match the
FBI had located. He'd been more than happy to
offer the information he had. Seven male cous-
ins. A nephew who was just five years old. A
grandfather. An uncle. Jessica was doing background searches on the adults, hoping to find
one who had connections in the medical field.
Currently, she was hunched over a computer,
staring at the screen.

Henry's in-laws had graciously offered to
let her and Wren stay the night. Saige and his
mother had been issued the same invitation. The
house was filled with people, most of them con-
gregated in the living room, discussing everything but the Molotov cocktail and the reason
why someone might have hired Tom to toss one
in the diner.

"Are you planning to go look for her?" Wren
asked. She'd taken a seat on the couch, her long
legs crossed neatly at the ankles, her suit still
wrinkle-free after hours of work. It was nearing

eight. She should be in her Boston apartment, enjoying her evening. Instead, she was in Provincetown helping him.

"I'm sorry for calling you out here like this, Wren. I know you have better things to do with your time."

"I can't think of any," she said with a quick smile.

"I can," Jessica intoned. "I had a hot date with the television and a microwave dinner."

"I've got something much nicer than that in the oven," Brett called from the kitchen. "Twenty minutes, and we'll have a nice lasagna, tossed salad and garlic bread. I also have a clam chowder on the stove, if anyone prefers that."

"Twenty minutes is enough time for me to swing by Tessa's place," Henry said. He had a bad feeling. One he couldn't shake. Kayla had dropped Tessa at her place a half hour ago. The officer had texted Henry to let him know that she'd watched her walk inside.

He'd been heading home from the police station, his SUV filled with people. It hadn't occurred to him that she wouldn't be okay.

Maybe it should have.

"I'll come with you," Wren said. "You don't mind staying here, do you, Jessica?"

"I'm good. I'm also hungry. If you're not back

quickly, I might eat both your shares of lasagna," she responded, her gaze still glued to the screen.

It was an idle threat.

When Jessica was on the trail of something, she didn't stop to eat. She barely stopped to sleep.

"How close are you?" Henry asked as he grabbed his coat from the closet.

"Very close," Jessica responded, not needing to ask what he meant. They'd both been working overtime, trying to catch the kidnapper before he struck again. "I may be able to pull some photo IDs from the national database. If so, we can use them tomorrow when the public defender arrives."

"That's great news," Wren commented, opening the front door and letting cold air sweep in. "But being close to finding the answer doesn't mean you shouldn't stop to eat and sleep."

"Right," Jessica agreed as she continued to stare at the computer screen.

"Maybe one of us should stick around and keep an eye on things while Jessica works," Henry suggested as he walked outside.

"Have you ever known Jessica to not be on top of a situation? Even when she's on a computer trail, she's at the top of her game," Wren responded.

"I know. But, the girls are prone to finding trouble, and Saige has a criminal charge against him."

"Your in-laws are exceptional at keeping your daughters out of trouble, and Saige is about as much of a criminal as an inchworm is a viper." Wren said, dashing to the SUV parked in the driveway and climbing in.

He followed, brushing frozen rain from his hair as he slid in behind the wheel. "He committed a crime."

"He was coerced by his father. He acted to save his mother. The first is a childish mistake. The last has some nobility in it."

"I'm surprised you think so, Wren. Usually you're pretty black-and-white about things," he said as they drove off.

"Usually, I'm not looking into the face of a fifteen-year-old kid whose mother is obviously dying," she replied, something in her voice making him look into her face. Really look.

Her hair was perfectly in place, her makeup understated and flawless. She looked as put-together as always, but she seemed more tired than usual, her eyes a deeper shade of brown, fine worry lines beneath them.

"Is everything okay?" he asked.

"With the case? I think we're on the right track."

"With you."

"I'm fine, Henry. Just caught up in this the same way you and Jessica are. It's been four weeks since Everly was taken from her room. The kidnapper has a history of striking every two or three months. The clock is ticking, and I'm worried he may strike sooner because he wasn't successful the last time."

"I've been worried about the same."

"I've been through the case files dozens of times. I've looked at the dates, the times of year, the places. I've run everything through every pattern-finding system I know, but there doesn't seem to be a pattern. That means there is no way of knowing where he might strike next."

"I'm thinking somewhere away from New England. All his victims have been in small towns in the northeast. He may head south or west."

"I agree."

"There's something else, Henry. Something I didn't want to say in front of the others."

"What?"

"It seems odd to me that the kidnapper has returned. He attempted to have Tessa murdered. He failed. Any one of the men he hired could identify him. Killing the lone witness to his crime will no longer solve his problems. Not the way disappearing will. If he stays away, the thugs he hired will go to jail. Tessa will go on with her life. He'll keep doing what he's doing in another location or in another way."

"We've discussed this at team meetings," he said, because they had. It was something they'd all been wondering and working through. If Jessica's criminal profile was correct, the kidnapper wasn't a risk-taker. The idea that he'd continue to stalk Tessa didn't make sense. Not when he'd gotten away free and clear.

"Thinking about that made me wonder if Tessa had any other enemies. I did a little digging into her life."

"That's a breach of privacy, Wren. She's not a criminal, and she's not a suspect in a crime."

"Maybe not, but someone seems to want her dead, and the easiest way to find out who is to figure out why."

"That's Deduction 101."

"And yet, you seem content to *not* go in that direction," Wren said.

"What's that supposed to mean?"

"I suspect that if Tessa were anyone else, you'd have already done a criminal background check on her. You haven't, because she rescued Everly, and you think you owe her privacy and a chance to come clean herself."

"Clean about what?"

"I don't know. The check came back with nothing. Except a death certificate."

"What?"

"Tessa Carlson. Twenty-nine years old. Light brown hair. Blue eyes."

"I'm familiar with her description."

"I doubt you know her social security number, but I pulled it off the most recent tax return she filed."

"And?"

"She died in a car accident ten years ago. She was nineteen."

He wanted to be surprised, but he wasn't.

He'd suspected Tessa was hiding something.

He shouldn't be disappointed to realize he'd been right.

Tessa had talked about being comfortable with him. She'd spoken about friendship. He'd felt both those things when he was with her. She was one of the few people he'd have trusted alone with his daughters. He'd told her that.

She'd repaid him by lying.

Or, at least, covering the truth.

"So, who is she?" he asked.

"We ran her prints. They're not in the system. I suspect she's a woman on the run from someone rather than a criminal on the run from the law."

"Are you planning to ask?" he said, shoving down the disappointment he knew he shouldn't be feeling. Tessa had helped Everly. That didn't make her a saint. The fact that she'd changed her identity didn't make her a criminal, either.

"I thought you should."

"Why?"

"You two are close. If she's going to tell anyone the truth, it's going to be you."

"She hasn't so far."

"Don't be bitter about it, Henry. There are plenty of people in this world who are hiding for very legitimate reasons." She frowned, leaning close to her window and peering into the icy downpour. "Someone is out there."

"Where?" he asked, slowing the SUV to a crawl.

"Between those houses."

"A dog maybe?"

"No. It's a person."

"I'll take a look," he said, pulling up to the curb and putting the SUV in Park. He needed a few minutes to cool off, to think through what he'd just found out and to try to make some sense of it.

"You don't know her reasons," Wren said. "Don't judge them until you do."

He knew she was still talking about Tessa.

He wasn't in the mood to listen.

He grabbed the Maglite from his glove compartment and climbed out of the SUV. The road was slippery, the grass covered with a layer of ice. Ice fell in sheets as he crossed a yard and stepped between a Victorian farmhouse and a 1920s bungalow. It was a frigid night, the temperature low enough to cause hypothermia relatively quickly. If someone was out there, he was either skulking around looking for trouble or confused about where he should be.

Henry focused the light on the patch of lawn between the houses. Several footprints were clearly visible, as the ice-coated grass had been pressed down.

"Who's out here?" he called.

"Henry?" Tessa responded, stepping around the corner of the bungalow. She had no coat. No gloves.

He ran toward her, shrugged out of his coat and threw it around her shoulders. Her hair was covered with a thick layer of ice, her skin was waxy and her lips were blue.

"You're freezing," he muttered, running his hands up and down the sleeves of the coat, trying to rub warmth into her through the fabric.

"I'll be okay."

"If your idea of being okay is being a snowman, then, yeah, you're going to be just fine," he muttered.

"I'd rather be a snowman than dead."

"What are you talking about?"

"Someone's at the cottage, Henry. He locked

me in the basement. I had to leave through the exterior door. I guess I got turned around when I ran onto the beach. I made it almost to the end of the peninsula before I realized my mistake."

"You're certain someone was in the cottage?"

"Would I be wandering around in the cold if I weren't?" she responded, her words slurred.

"Come on. You need to warm up."

"I need to figure out if it's Patrick," she replied.

The words made him pause, and if the weather had been nice, if she hadn't been nearly frozen, he'd have asked her to explain.

Instead, he scooped her up, carrying her back to the SUV.

She didn't protest.

That concerned him almost as much as the fact that she wasn't shivering.

"Everything okay?" Wren asked, running around the side of the vehicle.

"She's freezing."

"Who?" she asked.

"Me," Tessa responded.

"What happened?" Wren asked, all business, all focus.

"I turned the wrong way when I got to the beach and took a longer walk than I intended. That's the short version."

"What's the long version?" Wren opened the

door on the front passenger side of the SUV. "Put her in the front. Let's see if we can warm her up. If not, we'll head to the ER."

"The long version is that someone was at her place, and she managed to escape."

"I don't know," Tessa replied. "I didn't see him. I don't even know where he was hiding. I checked every room in the house before I went into the basement."

"Were you worried that someone was there?" Wren asked.

"I had a weird feeling that things were…off."

"You should have called me," Henry said.

"I tried to call you several times today. You weren't available," Tessa muttered, her eyes closed, her dark lashes coated with ice. Just like her hair. He turned up the heat and aimed the front vents directly at her.

"Then you should have called the police," he responded.

"I felt like something was off. I had no proof, and with everything that has happened lately, I couldn't be certain it wasn't my imagination."

"Always trust your gut," Wren said.

"My gut has been wrong one too many times, and I stopped trusting anything it told me a long time ago," Tess replied.

There was a story there. Probably the one

she'd been refusing to tell him. Henry didn't ask. Not yet. He had other things to focus on.

"I'll bring you two back to my in-laws. Then I'm going over to the cottage."

"Better to go now," Wren replied. "I'll call the chief and have him meet us there. Maybe we'll hit the lottery and the perp will be standing around waiting for us to arrive."

"Wouldn't that be nice?" Tessa asked, her eyes still closed, her hands fisted in her lap.

He lifted one. He meant to simply will some warmth into her skin, but he found himself giving it a gentle squeeze.

She opened her eyes, met his gaze, offered a tired smile that made him wish he could change all the things in her past that had made her doubt herself.

"I need to tell you some things about my life," she said. "I was thinking about that while I was nearly freezing to death out on the beach."

"Thinking about what?"

"All the things I should have said but didn't."

"There will be time to say them later," he said, and she nodded.

"I know. But, just in case you find out before they're said, I want you to know that I'm ready."

"For what?"

"To break the silence, to say everything I

should have said a hundred years ago," she responded and closed her eyes again.

She didn't open them when Henry brushed moisture from her hair. She didn't move as he pulled away from the curb. When they reached the cottage, her eyes were still closed, whatever story she planned to tell locked tightly behind her placid expression.

# EIGHT

The cottage had been ransacked. Boxes dumped. Papers strewn everywhere. Couch cushions sliced open to reveal their fluffy innards. Her schoolbooks were on the floor, scattered like trash through the dining room. Tessa reached for one, but Henry stepped in front of her, preventing her from touching it.

"Don't. When the evidence techs arrive, they'll want to take photos of an undisturbed scene."

"Is moving one book really going to matter?" she replied.

"Maybe not, but why take chances?"

"I have that makeup test on—"

"Monday," he said, because she'd mentioned it before. Just like she mentioned her dreams of finishing college, of getting her nursing degree and passing the national RN exam.

What she *hadn't* mentioned was why it had taken her until she was nearly thirty to pursue those dreams.

"I know I've told you about the test before," she said. She could feel her cheeks go pink with embarrassment. "I need to stop repeating myself."

"You need to keep that coat buttoned," he responded, tugging his coat tighter around her shoulders.

"I need to…" She shook her head.

"What?"

"Pass the test," she responded with a quick grin. Even she could see the humor in her answer, in the nearly obsessive way she focused on one of the few things she could control.

"You will," Wren assured her. "The police will process the scene, and we'll make sure you get your books back quickly." She'd taken position at the living room window. The curtains were open, and she was staring out into the freezing rain. She'd just returned to the house after checking the exterior of the house.

She didn't look happy.

"What's wrong?" Henry asked.

"I found a few footprints in the yard," she commented. "The cellar door was opened. The exterior lock was cut. I found it lying under a bush near the back stoop."

"That explains how he got in," Tessa murmured. "But I checked the house when I arrived home. I know it was empty. Maybe he broke in while I was in the basement, but I don't think he had enough time."

"Why not?" Henry asked.

"I walked to the bottom of the stairs, and the door closed. He locked me in, and a few seconds later, he shut off the electricity."

"He could have killed you, if he'd wanted to, so that couldn't have been his motive for breaking in." Henry crouched near one of the corner hutches and studied a handful of heart-shaped rocks that had been tossed on the floor. "It seems like he was searching for something."

"What?" she asked, even though her gut was telling her she knew.

"You're the only one who can answer that question." He'd been in the cottage before. He'd seen the collection of heart-shaped rocks, but he'd never commented on them. Now, he poked at one with the end of the Maglite he'd carried from the SUV. "You had a couple dozen of these."

"Yes."

"Where are the rest?"

"I don't know. Maybe under the papers?"

"No." He lifted a few sheets with the edge of the light and let them fall back into place. "We'd be able to see them."

"Like I said, I don't know."

"Heart-shaped stones are a strange thing to take, don't you think?"

"Everything about this is strange," she murmured.

She was used to Henry's warmth, to his kindness.

Now, he seemed coldly focused.

"There's a crawl space above the house. Where's the access point?"

"In my bedroom closet, but I never use it."

"That doesn't mean it wasn't used."

"You think someone was in the crawl space when I checked the house?" She'd thought about the basement, but the crawl space had never entered her mind.

"This is not a big place. There aren't many other places to hide." He straightened. "Aside from the rocks, does anything appear to be missing?"

Right. That's what she was supposed to be doing. Checking to see if she'd been robbed.

"My laptop is still here." She pointed to where it sat on the floor. "Other than the stones, everything seems to be here."

"So, nothing is missing from the living room. Nothing from the dining room. Want to check the kitchen next?"

"I don't have anything in there worth stealing," she said wearily.

"How about your bedroom?"

"As far as I'm concerned, there's nothing in this house that anyone would possibly want."

"What about information?" Henry suggested, and she stiffened.

"That's possible." She wasn't going to lie. She'd done enough of that when she'd lived with Patrick. She'd lied about her age to his friends. She'd lied about her level of happiness. She'd lied about the bruises when doctors noticed. She'd lied about Patrick being a great boyfriend and a wonderful person, about having money and freedom and the easy life all Patrick's associates valued.

She'd continued to lie after she'd left Napa Valley.

Her new life was built on one lie after another, and she wanted to change that. Even if it meant going to jail. She'd thought about that a lot when she was on the beach, cold wind seeping deep into her bones. About how she could die, and no one would know who she really was. No one would know her deepest truths.

"What kind of information?" he asked, and she had the strange feeling he knew the truth, that somehow, he'd discovered that she wasn't Tessa Carlson.

At least, not the real one.

She wanted to tell him about the twenty-six years she'd spent before she'd become the woman who lived in Provincetown. She wanted to tell him about her desperation to make something good out of her life. She wanted to explain how she'd met Patrick, how quickly she'd fallen for his charm, how all of it had been a sham, and she'd become trapped in a life she'd hated with a man she'd feared.

"Tessa, I can't help you, if you don't tell me the truth." He spoke calmly, no hint of emotion in his voice, but the coldness in his eyes brought back memories she tried hard to suppress—Patrick staring at her across the dinner table, asking calmly where she'd been when he'd returned from work, his gaze dispassionate and cold. Patrick asking why she was wearing blue instead of green. Why she'd taken out her contacts. Why she hadn't run to the door to greet him.

Always with that look in his eyes.

As if it didn't matter.

But, of course, it had mattered a lot.

"I'll check the bedroom," she murmured, but he was blocking the path to the hall, and she'd have to brush past him to get there.

She stayed where she was, her feet burning as they thawed, her finger aching.

It was her heart, though, that hurt the most.

She'd been hoping for something she hadn't been willing to put a name to. Family, maybe. Love.

Mostly she thought she'd just been hoping to have what Henry had been giving her. Easy conversations and relaxed meals. Quick smiles and loud laughter. Life without apology or fear, shared with someone she liked.

Her lies had ruined that.

She could see the truth in his mist-colored eyes.

He reached for her, and she flinched, taking two quick steps back before she realized what she was doing.

"The coat is slipping," he said in the same calm tone.

He tugged it into place again, buttoning the first few buttons and pulling the hood over her wet hair.

"Whatever you need to say, it's going to be okay," he promised, and she knew this was her last chance. She could either come clean, or she could wait for Henry and his colleagues to discover the truth.

Either way, all the lies she'd told, all the secrets she'd kept, were going to be exposed.

"I'm not, or wasn't, Tessa Carlson," she finally admitted, her heart racing, her chest so tight, she could barely breathe.

"Who are you, then?"

"Me. The person who rents this house and

works at the diner and is trying to become a nurse."

"Who *were* you?" Wren asked, turning away from the window she'd been staring out.

"Tiffany Freeman. I changed my name when I left California."

"Not legally?" Wren asked.

"No. Not legally."

"Why—?" Henry began.

"Did I change my name?" Tessa interrupted. "Because I was leaving a bad relationship. I didn't want him to find me. I was afraid, and I panicked, and I did what I thought I had to."

"Why didn't you tell me this before?" he asked gently, and she could feel tears burning behind her eyes. Her fingers tingled as blood flowed back into them, and she wanted to lean her head against his chest, close her eyes and pretend she hadn't made the biggest mistake of her life when she'd withheld the truth when they'd met.

"I was afraid. I'm always afraid."

"Not anymore," Wren insisted. "Now, it's out in the open. The only person who should be afraid is whoever has been coming after you. Who was it you were running from?"

"Patrick Dwight Hamilton. He owns several upscale antiques stores in Napa Valley and two in Los Angeles."

"He was your boyfriend," Henry said, because she had mentioned Patrick before. She just hadn't mentioned everything else.

"Right."

"For how long?"

"Nine years. I should have walked away after the first one, but I was young when we met, and I didn't know how."

"You don't have to explain," Henry said. "Do you think he might have come after you? Is it possible that everything we've attributed to the kidnapper, could be something to do with him?"

"I...don't know. He started dating right after I left. He's married. He's financially well-off, and he has no reason to come after me."

"Except?" Henry prodded, obviously sensing that there was more.

"He hates to lose at anything. He hates to be humiliated, and when his young, stupid girl-friend walked out, that had to have bothered him. Also, I took some things from his wall safe."

"What things?" Wren asked.

"He'd given me a lot of expensive jewelry, but he kept it in a safe in his closet. One day, I watched him open it and memorized the com-bination. Before I left, I took everything I found there. Some of it wasn't mine."

"What are we talking about here?" Henry asked. "A few hundred dollars' worth of stuff?"

"Tens of thousands worth. Maybe a quarter of that had been gifted to me. The rest were pieces he'd bought from estate sales and was waiting to get authenticated. He liked to take things home and admire them for a while before he displayed them in one of his stores. I knew that, and I knew that I was taking items that weren't mine. I did it anyway," she admitted, her cheeks hot with embarrassment. She was a thief, a common criminal.

Just like her mother.

"Did you sell the jewelry to fund your escape?" Wren asked. "New identities aren't cheap. Neither are trips across the country."

"Only the things that Patrick had given me. I contacted a guy I'd gone to school with, and he was able to help me get what I needed."

"What about the other things?" Henry asked.

She'd been avoiding his eyes, but she forced herself to meet his gaze. "They're in a safe-deposit box in Provincetown Savings and Loan. The key is here." She walked to one of the built-in hutches and kneeled on the floor. There was a small ledge that created a decorative feature. The key was taped behind it. She pulled it off and stood. "I haven't actually opened the box since I put the jewelry inside it. It's been there since I got the job at Ernie's. I wanted to send everything back, but…"

"You were afraid he'd find you," Henry said.

It wasn't a question, but she nodded.

"Right. I've been terrified of that since I left. The night Everly was kidnapped, I almost didn't intervene, because I didn't want any police attention. I built this life on a lie, but I loved it enough to want to keep it. I wish I could change the past and unmake a million mistakes, but I can't." The words poured out, and she wasn't sorry for telling him the truth.

All she felt was tired.

"You did what you thought you had to," Henry said, pity in his voice and in his eyes.

Somehow that was worse than his coldness had been.

"I need to check my room," she muttered, brushing past him and walking down the hall.

Henry followed Tessa to her room.

He would have followed her into it, but Wren grabbed his arm and pulled him up short.

"I got a text from Jessica while I was outside."

"About?"

"She has a name."

It took a minute for the words to register. When they did, he wanted to shout a million praises. "Who?"

"Guy named William Stevenson. Zebedee Cantor's cousin. Thirty years old. Degree in business. He has partial ownership in an event company that plans fund-raisers and parties."

"He's local to New England?"

"Lives in Saugus. I'm sending Anderson Jeffries out with a warrant to search his house and obtain a DNA sample. He'll be transported to the field office for questioning."

"He's our guy," Henry said. "I'm sure of it."

"Being sure isn't proof. We'll gather what we need, and then we'll make the arrest. What we won't be doing is letting him wander around free while we're getting what we need. I'm going outside to make a few phone calls. Maybe you should check on Tessa now."

She walked away, and he glanced in the room.

Tessa was standing next to the bed, sheets and blanket on the floor near her feet, a pillow torn apart and lying in the middle of the shredded mattress. Books and clothes were strewn across the room, and a bookshelf had been knocked over.

He should have been collecting the details, filing them away in his mind to dissect later. Instead, he was noticing that Tessa had shoved her hands into his coat pockets, and that she was nearly dwarfed by the down parka, the hem hitting her just below the knees.

She must have sensed his gaze. She met his eyes, tried to smile. "It's a mess."

"Messes are easy to clean."

"Not the one I've made of my life."

"You haven't made a mess of it."

"I have. Or, I had. I'm trying to make things right. That's what I've spent the last few years doing. Making amends to myself for all the stuff I did wrong," Tessa explained. Her teeth had stopped chattering, and she wasn't trembling. Her core body temperature was obviously going up, but she was pale as paper, her lips colorless. "This was Patrick's doing, Henry. Wren said I should always listen to my gut, and if I do that, I know the truth."

"It took him a long time to find you."

"I don't know that he cared to, but my photo was in a couple of news reports. I saw it, and if I did, Patrick might have. He watched the news every morning before he left for work."

Henry had seen the photo, too. Everly's name and photo had been kept private because she was a minor, but a blurry photo of Tessa had been splashed across national news stations for a week. She had refused interviews and ducked away from cameras, but she hadn't been able to avoid being named as part of one of the biggest news stories of the year.

Now, he understood her reluctance to exploit her five minutes of fame.

What he didn't understand was why she hadn't told him the truth.

He'd given her plenty of opportunities, he'd asked plenty of questions. He'd given her every reason to trust him and to trust the system. He pushed aside disappointment and frustration. There wasn't time for either of those emotions. No matter who Tessa was, no matter what she'd run from, she'd saved Everly's life. He wasn't going to allow her to lose hers because of it.

Someone knocked on the front door, and he took her arm.

"We have a possible suspect for the kidnapping, Tessa. One of our agents is going to find him. From what we can tell, he's currently at his home in Saugus."

"Not in Provincetown stalking me," she said. "So, I was right. This is Patrick's doing."

"Maybe. Probably. One way or another, we're going to find out. You're not alone anymore, Tessa. You don't have to be afraid. You have a bunch of people standing beside you, fighting with you. Trust in that, and in God. Everything really will be okay."

He led her out of the destroyed room.

Chief Simpson was standing in the living room, ice on his hair and his shoulders. "I got a call that there was some trouble out here. I can see that was an understatement. Are you okay, Tessa?"

"Yes," Tessa murmured, her face still colorless.

"I suppose you two have a theory for what's going on here?" he said, meeting Wren's eyes and then Henry's.

Henry explained quickly and succinctly.

When he finished, the chief frowned.

"So, you want me to believe that this is about old jewelry that was taken more than three years ago?" he asked, his gaze dropping to the destroyed pillows and the cotton stuffing that was strewn across the room.

"Not just old jewelry. Patrick sold expensive estate items. He once sold a ten-million-dollar ring to someone in Hollywood," Tessa offered.

"Must have been a very fancy ring," Simpson said. "What did you take from his safe? The ruby slippers from *The Wizard of Oz*? A crown worn by Princess Grace?" The questions were nearly flip in their terseness, but he called in a request for a patrol car at the savings and loan before Tessa could answer.

When he finished, he ran his hand over thick salt-and-pepper hair. "You've gotten yourself into quite a mess, Tessa."

"I know."

"But being in a mess doesn't mean staying

in one. If your friends will drive you over to the bank, I'll have the owner, Orlando Smithson, open the place up for you. He'll be grumpy about it, but we're hunting buddies, and he's not going to say no. I think we need to look at what you stole...took from the safe. Maybe there's something in it worth more than money."

That was exactly what Henry had been thinking.

"I really do appreciate this, Chief Simpson," Tessa said.

"Thank me by getting this cleared up. I don't like trouble in my town, and I don't like troublemakers."

"I've never tried to be one," she responded, and he shook his head.

"You never have been one, but you sure are attracting them to the area. The kidnapper—"

"That had nothing to do with her," Henry pointed out.

"The Molotov cocktail this morning. Now this. What's next?"

"Hopefully answers to a lot of questions," Wren said, stepping back inside. "I made a call to our Los Angeles field office and asked for any information regarding Patrick Hamilton. I'm curious to see if he has been on their radar for any reason. I'd also like to know what he has been up to these past few years. I plan to do a background check and contact the LA police department. That will be easier to do at headquarters. If you two can handle things here, I'll walk back to the Halifax place. The weather is going to be horrible all weekend. Maybe the girls would rather spend their time in Boston?" She met Henry's eyes. "I could escort your in-laws and the girls to your place, suggest that they go to the children's museum tomorrow and, maybe, get ice cream afterward. That would give them some fun things to do until the weather clears."

*And, it will get them away from the danger.*

She didn't add the rest.

She didn't need to.

Desperate people did desperate things, and Patrick Hamilton seemed desperate to recover whatever it was he'd lost. Henry didn't want the twins anywhere nearby if he came calling.

"Great idea. How about we drop you off at the house before we go to the savings and loan? That way I can explain things to everyone."

"Whatever works for you," Wren said.

"It's fine if you plan to drop her off, but I suggest you not take too long doing it. Orlando is not going to be happy if you make him wait," the chief warned.

The girls weren't going to be happy, either.

They'd expected a fun-filled weekend on the Cape, spending time with their new favorite person. Tessa had entered their lives, and the girls seemed to believe that she would always be there.

But that wasn't the way life worked.

People didn't always stay.

And when it came to people with pasts like Tessa's, they often didn't.

He'd explain that to the girls when this was over and they'd all moved on with their lives.

# NINE

Provincetown Savings and Loan was on the northern edge of town, set apart from the touristy areas and still sitting in the center of the eighty-acre lot that banker Gerald Smithson had purchased nearly seventy years ago. There were a few houses nearby, tucked into a tidy court that had been paved and built after Gerald had finally agreed to sell sixty acres of his property to a developer. His only child, Orlando, lived on what remained—a 40-by-300 slice of land that backed up to the bank's parking lot.

Tessa hadn't been around when the sale had taken place, but Vera, the sixty-five-year-old bank teller who'd been working at Provincetown Savings and Loan since the 1970s, had told her all about it. She'd also told Tessa that Orlando had never forgiven his father for selling the property and spending the money on a retirement home in Florida. Nor had he forgiven him for willing Orlando the bank with the stipulation that it never be sold outside the family. Orlando had three children. None of them were interested in running the savings and loan.

Tessa had spent enough time with Orlando to understand why.

He was a mean and crusty version of Santa Claus. White beard and mustache, red cheeks, big belly and blue eyes, he smoked like a chimney and drank like a fish. His least favorite thing to do, it seemed, was talk to people.

He wasn't going to be happy about being asked to open the place at nine o'clock at night.

Tessa could see him as Henry pulled into the nearly empty parking lot, a yellow parka pulled over what looked like flannel pajamas, a hood covering his white hair but not hiding his irritated expression. A uniformed police officer stood a few feet away, not looking at Orlando and not speaking to him. Jessica was beside him, tapping her foot impatiently, waiting for them to arrive. Wren must have asked her to come.

"Hurry it up!" Orlando yelled as they got out of the SUV. "I'm in the middle of watching my programming, and you're making me miss it."

"Sorry about this, Mr. Smithson," Tessa replied, nearly running across the slippery parking lot in her hurry to reach him. Her foot slid as she stepped onto the ice-coated cement sidewalk in front of the building, and she would have fallen if Henry hadn't grabbed her arm.

"Careful," he said, not releasing her as Orlando used three keys to unlock the door, then rushed inside to disarm the alarm.

"I'm not sure what the all-fire hurry is, Tessa," Orlando griped. "You've got six days a week you can come in here and get a look in that box, and suddenly, nine o'clock on a Friday night rolls around, and you decided you need to see it now."

He pushed down his hood and stomped across the lobby, his winter boots leaving wet splotches on the carpet.

"I know this is a bother, sir, but it really is an emergency," Henry interjected.

Orlando whirled around, fire in his eyes and a scowl on his face. "Your created crisis isn't my problem, young man."

"I'm Special Agent Henry Miller. My associate and I are with the FBI." He gestured toward Jessica, who'd stepped into the bank behind them. The uniformed officer had, probably wisely, waited outside.

"They let women in the FBI now, huh?" Orlando said, turning away and finishing his trek to a metal door marked with an employees-only sign.

"They have been doing that for a long time, Mr. Smithson," Jessica responded without any heat in her voice. She'd probably taken classes on how not to become enraged by rude people.

"Good to know," he replied. "I got me a granddaughter who wants to be a police officer. I think the FBI has got more money in it for her, and I'd venture, a better retirement plan. What do you say? Is that true?" He fished a key ring from his pocket and fumbled through dozens of keys until he found the one he wanted.

"Maybe, but money shouldn't be the main reason for pursuing a career."

Orlando snorted. "Says a young woman who's wearing two-hundred-dollar boots."

"Says an elderly man who knows what a two-hundred-dollar pair of boots looks like," Jessica responded.

Orlando howled with laughter. "You've got a brain in your head, Ms. FBI Agent."

"And you've got an eye for nice footwear."

"My Dora loved shoes. May God rest her shoe-hoarding soul. She left a closet full when she passed seven years ago. I ended up selling them on eBay. Twisted Sisters thrift store wouldn't take them off my hands because they were too pricey for local blood." He shoved a key into the lock and turned it. The door swung open, and he flicked on the light in a narrow hallway.

He unlocked a second door and ushered them

into a room with floor-to-ceiling safe-deposit boxes. "All right. So, you are number what, Tessa?"

She pulled the key from her pocket and read the number engraved on it. "Two twenty-five."

"One of our smaller ones. This way." He stomped across the room and pointed to a box smack-dab in the middle of the wall. Tessa remembered it from three years ago. This time, her hands weren't shaking when she turned the key in the lock, and she wasn't trying to hide the cloth-wrapped jewelry as she took all of it out of the box.

She handed Henry the pieces one at a time, and he carried them to a small table that sat in the middle of the room.

There was more than she remembered. Fifteen pieces. Mostly small boxes that she'd wrapped in pieces of a flowery silk dress.

She'd hated that dress, and she hated looking at proof of who she'd been.

Who she still was.

Just because she'd purchased a new identity didn't mean she'd become a new person. She'd allowed herself to forget that for a while.

"Do you want to unwrap them, or do you want me to?" Henry asked, his eyes boring into hers. She knew he was upset, and she didn't blame him. She'd lied to him, to his family, to everyone in Provincetown.

"I'll do it." She lifted the first box and pulled off the rubber band, releasing the silk it held in place and opening the box it contained.

She did the same with the remainder, finally stopping when she unwrapped a beautiful gold watch. She set it carefully on the table and stepped back. Ten rings. Two bracelets. Two necklaces. A set of gold cuff links. A watch.

"Whoa! Tessa! You've got quite a haul there," Orlando crowed. "What'd you do? Rob a bank?" He cackled gleefully.

No one else was laughing.

The jewelry had to be worth a small fortune, and the watch was probably real gold. She'd stolen enough to qualify for a federal charge. That was for sure.

"Kind of interesting," Orlando said, moving closer to the table.

"What?" she asked, wishing she could bundle everything up and shove it into the safe-deposit box again.

"You've got all those beautiful old pieces." He pointed to one of the rings. "That is a mourning ring. Eighteenth century. Probably twenty-four-karat gold. Real sapphires and rubies in the flower. Not those fake ones that are made in labs."

"Your wife collected antique jewelry, too?" Jessica asked.

"My mother did. I still have a lot of her pieces. Got one a lot like that." He pointed to a diamond tennis bracelet. "From the 1940s. Mine-cut. Probably worth ten thousand on a bad day. Seems like you've got some really good taste and some really fine pieces, and then you've got that." He jabbed his finger at the watch.

"What about it?" she asked.

"It's a watch."

"A nice one," Henry pointed out.

"That's an understatement," Orlando said with a soft snort. "That's a Rolex. I don't know much about them, but I know they cost money. I also think that's modern, and I'm wondering why you'd ruin a perfectly good antique jewelry collection with a modern piece."

"That's a good question," Tessa said, lifting the watch. She hadn't touched it in over three years, and she'd forgotten how heavy it was.

"Well, it's your collection, Tessa," Orlando said. "You're the one who should be answering it."

"Right." But, of course, she couldn't. She had no idea why Patrick had been keeping the Rolex in the house safe. He didn't deal in antique watches. That was something she'd heard him discuss with clients and with friends they had over for dinner. She'd often picked at her plate of food while he and his business partner, Ryan Wilder, entertained some of their wealthier customers.

Unlike Patrick, Ryan had always tried to include Tessa in the conversations. His wife had been the same. Sheila had been down-to-earth and easy to talk to, her unapologetic laughter always making Tessa smile. The fact that she'd married Patrick wasn't a surprise, though. They'd had everything in common—age, sophistication, and love of fine wine, good food and expensive clothes.

Still, Tessa had expected Sheila to mourn for a lot longer than the year and a half it had taken her to get engaged to her deceased husband's business partner. Maybe she'd been lonely and looking for someone to fill the emptiness. She'd loved Ryan the way Tessa had wanted to be loved. A month before he was murdered in a botched burglary attempt at the Los Angeles antiques store, Sheila had thrown him a surprise birthday party. It had been his forty-fifth, and he'd arrived dressed in worn jeans, a sweatshirt and a pair of scuffed running shoes.

No one had commented on the casual clothes. That had struck Tessa, because she'd been forced to wear five-inch black stilettos and a perfectly fitted cocktail dress. Patrick had made her change outfits three times before they'd left for the venue—a country club a few miles from their home—because she'd needed to "live up to the standard of the people she'd be dining with."

The standard Ryan had set was much more her style, but when he'd walked into the reserved ballroom, Tessa had braced to hear complaints from Sheila. Instead, Sheila had thrown her arms around him and told him how fabulous he looked for a man of his advanced age.

Everyone had laughed.

Except for Patrick.

Later, when Sheila had presented Ryan with his gift, she hadn't seemed to care that his outfit hadn't matched the expensive Rolex.

Tessa frowned.

Ryan's watch had looked a lot like the one she was holding. As a matter of fact, if she didn't know better, she would have thought they were the same.

But, of course, they couldn't be.

Ryan's watch had been stolen the night he'd been murdered. As far as she knew, it hadn't been recovered. Plus, it had been engraved. He'd passed it around at the dinner party so that everyone could read the inscription.

She flipped the watch over, her heart skipping a beat as she saw the words on the back casing.

*Until forever ceases to exist, I'll love you.*

"That's strange," she murmured, flipping it over again as if that would someone explain what she'd seen.

"What is?" Henry asked.

"This watch is engraved."

"Lots of watches are," Orlando replied. "There's nothing strange about it, and as much as I've enjoyed seeing all those fine pieces, I *am* missing my shows. Are you taking those things with you, or putting them back? If it were me, I'd lock them up again, but…not my choice."

"Is there a reason why the engraving is strange?" Henry asked, ignoring Orlando's comment.

"This belonged to Patrick's business partner. Ryan Wilder. He was killed several months before I left Napa Valley."

"Killed in an accident? Or murdered?"

"Murdered. In a botched robbery attempt at the antiques store in Los Angeles. That store was his baby. The ones in Napa Valley were more Patrick's. Ryan told his wife, Sheila, that he had to work on inventory and left their town house around ten that night. The police think he surprised a burglar."

"Did his wife give Patrick the watch as a token to remember Ryan by?" Jessica asked.

"To be honest, I thought Sheila told me it had been stolen. The store lost around fifty thousand dollars' worth of items. More would have been taken, but the thief broke secured display cases and set off an alarm."

"If it was stolen, how did it end up here?" Jessica took it from her hand and flipped it so that she could read the inscription.

"It couldn't have. I'm probably mistaken about it being stolen. That's all." She closed all the boxes and stacked them in the safe-deposit box, then held out her hand for the watch. "I'd better put that back, too. I'll have to return everything to Patrick, and I don't want to lose any of it before then."

"Hold on. I want to snap a photo of it." Jessica pulled out her cell phone and snapped several pictures, then wrapped the watch in a piece of silk and handed it to Tessa.

"Thanks." She locked the safe-deposit box, uneasy and anxious and not sure why.

By the time they walked out, she'd almost convinced herself that she was tired and overly emotional, that seeing the jewelry had sent her back to a place she preferred not to visit, and that going there had muddled her memory.

*You're tired.*

*You're too emotional.*

*You've scrambled things in your brain.*

She could hear Patrick's words whispering through her mind, the phrases so often repeated when they were together that she'd begun to believe them.

But she'd been away from him for years. In all that time, no one had ever called her too emotional or accused her of scrambling information she'd been given.

She was a straight-A college student. She managed a diner. She hadn't become less smart or less capable because she was tired and stressed.

"What are you thinking about?" Henry asked as he held open the door and waited for her to climb into the SUV.

"That I'm not mistaken. Sheila told me the watch was taken the night of the murder."

"Then maybe that watch is the thing Patrick is trying to get back." He closed the door, and she heard him call out to Orlando, offering him a ride to his house.

She didn't hear Orlando's reply.

She didn't have to.

Orlando would refuse.

That was just the way he was. Crusty and grumpy, but smarter and kinder than she'd thought.

Patrick had been the opposite. Handsome and charismatic, but shrewder and more sinister than she ever could have imagined.

Ryan's watch had been in Patrick's safe.

There was a reason for that, and Tessa didn't think it was a good one.

Was it possible he'd had something do with Ryan's death?

She didn't want to believe it.

But then, she hadn't wanted to believe that he would throw a vase at her again, strangle her again, hit her again.

He'd done all those things.

Could he have murdered his partner, too?

Wren called with an update as Henry exited the parking lot. Anderson Jeffries and two other agents had taken William Stevenson into custody without incident. He was at the field office, waiting to be questioned while they searched his house. They'd already discovered a cache of child pornography, and she felt strongly that he was the serial kidnapper.

She was driving Rachelle and the girls back to Boston. Brett had opted to stay behind to keep an eye on their guests. Saige's mother still wasn't feeling well, and he was worried she'd need a ride to the ER.

That was typical of Brett. He went out of his way for others. Rachelle was the same. Diane had been, too. They lived their faith in a way Henry admired. Even in the darkest time of their lives, Rachelle and Brett hadn't questioned

God's goodness. Days after Diane's death, they'd visited the mother of the young man who'd killed her. The drive-by shooting had been gang-related. Diane had been in the wrong place at the wrong time—standing at the bus stop waiting for transportation to the inner-city school where she'd taught. The gunman had been a sixteen-year-old punk, and his mother had been devastated when she realized what he'd done.

So, Rachelle and Brett had visited with her. They'd prayed with her. They'd offered her words of encouragement and comfort.

Henry had been at the hospital with the girls.

Even if he hadn't been, he doubted he'd have had it in him to do what they had. He'd had no sympathy when the kid had been tried as an adult, and he'd felt no remorse when the judge handed down a life sentence.

If someone committed a crime, then there had to be consequences. He'd gone into law enforcement to protect the innocent and to make certain the guilty were taken off the street.

Tessa had stolen jewelry from her ex.

That was a criminal offense.

If she was prosecuted for and convicted of grand theft, she could face up to five years in prison. She'd get more time if she was convicted of identity theft. He wanted to feel okay with that.

But just as Saige's story had made him want to fight for the teen's freedom, Tessa's made him want to fight for her. She'd been only eighteen when she'd met Patrick. She'd been abused, mistreated and terrorized.

She'd left because she'd had no choice.

She'd changed her name because she'd been afraid.

She'd taken what she could get her hands on, because she'd had nothing.

He couldn't judge her for that, and he couldn't find her guilty of anything other than being young and alone.

"What now?" she asked when he finished his conversation with Wren.

"We're going to get in touch with Patrick and see what he has to say about things."

She tensed, and it reminded him of the way she'd flinched when he'd reached for her back at the house.

"It will be okay," he said, because he would make certain it was.

"You don't know Patrick. He's…very good at pretending to be everything he's not."

"We meet plenty of people like him, Tessa. You've got nothing to worry about," Jessica assured her from the backseat of the SUV. She had her cell phone in hand and was sending texts. Henry imagined they were to the field office.

She probably wished she could have been there when Stevenson arrived, but she wouldn't say as much.

"That's pretty much what I thought the day I met him. I was very, very wrong." She leaned her forehead against the window, and Henry could almost feel her regret.

"It can't be easy letting us see into your life. We understand that, but if Patrick is the one who broke into your house—"

"It wasn't him. I caught a glimpse of the guy when he walked out of the cottage. He was taller and broader than Patrick."

"It's been three years. People gain weight," Jessica pointed out.

"He didn't move the same way. Patrick always walked with confidence. The guy I saw lumbered."

"It could be someone he hired to find the watch," Henry said.

"If the watch is what he wants."

"What else could it be?" Jessica tapped her fingers against the back of the seat. "He isn't the sort of guy who'd ruin a perfectly good life of wealth to get revenge. At least, based on what you've told us, he isn't."

"Why do you say that?" Henry asked.

"Because he waited three years. If he'd been after Tessa for the sake of revenge or the sake of regaining some form of control, he'd have found her before now. My hunch is, he saw her on the news, and he started thinking about that watch, wondering if she'd sold it, kept it or even knew what she had. Maybe he felt compelled to look, because his life is going exactly the way he planned, and he didn't want it messed up if Tessa suddenly decided to come forward with proof of his crimes."

"You're assuming he murdered his partner. Or had something to do with it."

"Aren't you?" Jessica asked.

"Yes."

"Were Patrick and Ryan friends before you met him, Tessa?" Jessica asked.

"Yes. They met at Stanford."

"Smart guys, huh?"

"Very. Patrick has a degree in business administration and a minor in antiquities. Ryan was a CPA. They decided to combine their strengths and open an antiques store together. I met Patrick about twelve years later. By that point, they had three storefronts."

"That's impressive."

"They had impressive lifestyles, too. Houses in Napa Valley and in Los Angeles. Nice cars. Country-club memberships."

"So, an expensive lifestyle?" Henry asked,

turning onto a side road that cut through the north section of town.

"Very."

"Were there ever any money problems?" he continued.

"I wouldn't have known. I was one of the pretty things Patrick collected. I didn't have access to information about finances. Why do you ask?"

"Money is a leading motive for murder. Do you think Patrick would have been capable of killing a guy he'd been friends with for two decades?"

"I...don't know."

"Do you know if anyone was arrested for the murder?"

"When I left, the murder was still being investigated, but Patrick wasn't a suspect. He was home with me at the time of the murder."

"Money buys a lot of things," Jessica said. "And the cost of a man's life isn't nearly as expensive as it should be."

That was the truth.

Henry had worked more than a few cases that involved hired hit men, and he'd often been astounded and bemused at how little value was put on a life.

"If Patrick paid a hit man, I'm sure the police would have figured it out by now."

"Not necessarily. He had a business. He had access to cash. If that's the way he paid, the police would have difficulty finding evidence of the payment," Henry said as fat flakes of snow splattered the window.

Faith Community Church was to the left, its white steeple spearing the gray-black sky. An old cemetery dotted the field next to it, wrought-iron gates preventing access after sundown. Henry had been there dozens of times during the day, driving down the paved road that cut through stretches of well-cared-for plots. Sometimes, the girls were with him. Sometimes, he went alone. Always, he drove to a beautiful maple, parked there and walked to Diane's grave.

He glanced at the gates as he passed. Just as he always did.

A car was idling there, exhaust puffing from the muffler, headlights off. He glanced in the rearview mirror as he reached the end of the street. The car had pulled out and was following, lights still off. Not trying to close the distance between them, but definitely heading in the same direction.

"We have company," he said, and both women turned to look out the back window.

"If he'd wanted to be subtle, he should have turned his lights on," Jessica murmured. "Do you want me to call for local help?"

"Let's make certain he's really on our tail." He eased off the accelerator and took the next turn. Seconds later, the car followed.

Another turn and another, and the guy was still behind them. No closer. No farther away. Lights still off. They were back where they'd started, slowly driving past the cemetery.

"You'd think he'd have a clue that we're on to him," Jessica said.

"Maybe he wants us to know he's here. Maybe he's hoping we'll stop for a chat. How about we give him what he wants?" Henry turned into the church parking lot, and the car passed, accelerating down the street and taking the turn at a dangerous pace for the conditions.

"He's gone," Tessa said with a note of relief in her voice.

"How about we test that theory?" Henry responded, putting the SUV in Park and stepping into the freezing rain and falling snow. "Pastor Walker always leaves the sanctuary door unlocked. Let's go in there for a few minutes."

"I'd rather go home," Tessa commented, her focus on the road.

"It's a crime scene, remember? I'm taking you to Brett and Rachelle's place for the night." He opened her door and tugged her out. She was still wearing his coat, and he didn't want to take it from her.

Instead, he opened the hatch of the SUV and grabbed the spare he kept there. Coat. Boots. Gloves. Clothes. Blankets. Food. He'd been stuck in a snowstorm in Boston a few years back, and he'd learned a good lesson about always being prepared for the weather.

"What are you doing?" Tessa asked as Jessica took her arm and steered her toward the church.

"Going hunting," he replied as he shut the hatch and slipped into the coat.

# TEN

Henry had obviously lost his mind, and Tessa would have been happy to tell him that if her throat hadn't been constricted with fear.

If Patrick was in that car...

But he couldn't be.

He was married. He had a life. He wouldn't have flown across the country to stalk and taunt her.

But he might have come for the Rolex.

No matter how much she tried to convince herself that he'd have never harmed Ryan, she couldn't make her heart believe it.

She knew what the handsome facade, the charming smile and the winning sense of humor hid. She'd seen the ugliness beneath the beauty so many times, she'd stopped being attracted to Patrick long before she'd left him.

"I don't think this is a good idea," she finally said as they reached the sanctuary door.

"Pastor Walker won't mind," Henry responded, and she knew he was being purposely obtuse.

"You know what I mean, Henry. We should have already called the police. Chief Simpson can deal with whomever is in the car, and we can go back to your in-laws' place."

She had no intention of staying there, of course.

She'd wrecked what she had with Brett and Rachelle, with the twins, and with Henry.

She'd brought trouble into the lives of people she'd come to care about, and she couldn't be anywhere near them until she was absolutely certain the danger had passed.

There was a hostel outside of town. It catered to free-spirited vagabonds who had Provincetown on their exploration bucket lists. This time of year, it was empty. She could get a room for cheap and for cash.

"I do, and maybe it seems like a risk, but I've been doing this for a while, Tessa. Everything will be fine."

"People say that every day, and every day, things go terribly wrong."

"Stay inside with Jessica. Keep away from the windows. I don't think this guy was gunning for you, but I don't want to take any chances." He nudged her into the dark vestibule, his hand resting on her back for just a moment.

She didn't turn, throw herself into his arms and beg him to stay, but she wanted to.

"What are you planning?" Jessica asked.

"A reconnaissance mission. Put a call into the chief. Ask to have his troopers arrive with lights and sirens off. I don't want to scare our friend."

He stepped back and let the door swing closed, plunging them into near-total darkness.

The exit sign above the door was the only light in the narrow entryway, and Jessica grabbed Tessa's wrist and tugged her a step closer. "Let's not get separated in this mausoleum."

"It's a church," Tessa said. "The sanctuary is through the door straight ahead of us."

"I take it you've been here before."

"Every Sunday for almost three years."

"What are the other entrance points?" Jessica asked, dragging her to the double doors that opened into the sanctuary.

"You mean aside from the windows?"

"Yes."

"There's a choir room at the back of the sanctuary. It has an exit door."

"Okay. I'll check to see if it's locked."

"Maybe we should go together," Tessa suggested.

"Are their windows in the choir room?"

"Yes."

"Then you'd better stay here."

"There are windows—" Tessa began, but Jessica had already walked away.

She could have followed, but icy rain was pelting the windows, bits of snow sticking to the exterior glass. She thought she saw a shadow walk past one, the darkness beyond shifting just enough to worry her.

"There's nothing to be afraid of," she said, her voice echoing in the empty room. On Sundays it was filled with worshippers, and light shimmered through the windows on either side of the long room and filtered in through a smaller window at the front. It felt warm then. Now it was cold, the chill seeping through her still-damp clothes.

The darkness beyond the window shifted again, and she moved closer to the vestibule door, trying to stay in deep shadows and out of sight of anyone who might be looking in.

"Door's locked," Jessica called, jogging toward her from the front of the room. She was in the center of the sanctuary when the vestibule doors flew open, knocking Tessa forward. She fell hard, skidding across the floor.

Someone grabbed her ponytail, yanking her backward when she tried to scramble away.

A knife pressed against the underside of her jaw, and she froze.

"Everyone just stay calm," a man said, the

words tickling the hair near her ear. "I'm not here to hurt anyone. I'm just here for what I'm due."

"What," Jessica asked, taking a step closer, "is that?"

"A few baubles to pay off a debt that's owed me," he replied. "Now how about you just back off, lady? If I get nervous, and the knife slips, someone could get hurt."

"How about you not do anything you'll regret?" Jessica replied. She had her firearm in one hand, and her phone in the other, her dark eyes gleaming through the gray-black darkness.

"I'm not going to regret this. I can tell you that much. According to my buddy, this lady has a small fortune. I just want a little piece of it. I'm assuming it's back at the bank I followed you to?" He gave Tessa a little shake, and she nodded.

"Fine. We'll go there, have your buddy open the door again and you give me what I came for. Once I have it, I'll go on my merry way."

More likely, once he had what he wanted, he'd kill her.

She didn't dare say what she was thinking.

Jessica sidled forward again, and the guy pressed the knife a little deeper. The blade nicked the skin beneath Tessa's jaw, and a bead of blood slid down her neck.

She didn't breathe.

She didn't swallow.

She was afraid to blink.

If she was killed, everything she'd worked for would be wasted.

"Lady, I told you to back off!" the man shouted, and Jessica shrugged.

"Fine. I'll stay here. You go outside. My partner is waiting for you there."

"You're lying."

"Try me and see." She tucked her firearm in the holster and folded her arms across her chest.

"Where's the other exit? I know there is one!" the man snarled, giving Tessa a little shake, the blade of the knife skipping across her throat.

It might have sliced the skin, but she didn't feel it.

She couldn't feel anything but the wild pounding of her heart.

"Behind the pulpit," she said, the words rattling like dry bones.

"Let's go." He dragged her sideways, his focus on Jessica.

"Patrick is just using you," Tessa said, her mouth cottony with fear, her mind racing.

Jessica hadn't made another move toward them, and that had to mean something. She was a trained law-enforcement officer. The FBI had rigorous physical requirements. If she'd wanted to, she could have made a move or taken a shot.

So, why wasn't she?

"I don't care who uses me so long as they're paying me well for the privilege."

"How much is he giving you?" Jessica asked. "A thousand? Two? What's a life worth on today's market?"

"I already told you, I'm not here to hurt anybody. I'm here to get what this lady stole from her friend." He dragged Tessa down the aisle near the windows. They were closing in on the pulpit. A few more feet and they'd be there, moving through the doorway in the back wall and heading for the exit.

She needed to free herself before then.

She glanced around, hoping that somewhere in the darkness of the sanctuary, she could find a weapon.

A shadow moved near the pulpit. At first, she thought she was seeing things. Then it moved again, sliding between choir chairs, slowly and soundlessly moving toward them.

"Did you kill Patrick's partner—Ryan? Was that your first job?" Jessica asked, and Tessa realized she was creating a distraction, attempting to keep the man's focus on something other than the front of the room and the shadow that was creeping closer.

"I don't know what you're talking about," the man said, an edge to his voice that made Tessa doubt him.

Was he Ryan's killer?

The thought sent cold rage shooting through her blood.

"Sure you do. You got paid to go into an antiques shop and murder an innocent man. You took a few things to make it look like a robbery and gave them to Patrick in exchange for the rest of your payment. I guess you didn't realize that the stuff you grabbed was worth way more than what he was paying."

"Shut up!" the man shouted.

"I don't think I have to," Jessica replied with a taunting lilt in her voice.

"I. Said. Shut. Up," the man screamed, so focused on Jessica he didn't see the person rising up from the floor behind him.

Tessa couldn't see a face or hair color, but she knew it was Henry. She could tell by the way he moved, quickly and silently, as he rushed toward an armed man without a thought for himself.

Terrified that he'd be hurt, she jerked sideways, grabbing a hymnal from the end of a pew and smashing it into the man's head. He cursed, tossing her backward. She slammed into the wall, her head banging into limestone, stars dancing at the edges of her vision.

She tried to move, but her body was uncoordinated, her movements clumsy. She had a quick glimpse of the knife slicing toward her through the darkness, and then Henry tackled the man from behind, and they both crashed to the floor.

The guy was big, and he was strong, but Henry was well-trained and angry. He managed to flip the perp onto his stomach and hike up the arm holding the knife behind his back.

The man yelped and the knife dropped from his fingers.

"You're going to break my arm, man!" he yelled.

"Stop struggling, and you won't have to worry about that," Jessica suggested, pulling handcuffs from beneath her jacket.

"This is all a misunderstanding. A prank gone wrong," the guy replied, still trying to free himself.

Henry yanked up his hand a little higher. "Pranks that involve knives and threats aren't funny."

"You can ask her ex. He'll tell you. He hired me to scare her a little. Teach her a lesson for leaving him like she did."

"And you were going to retrieve a few things for him while you were at it?" Henry accepted the cuffs from Jessica and snapped them on, then pulled the guy to his feet.

"I was doing what he asked me to."

"What he paid you to do?" Jessica suggested.

"What's it matter?"

"Police!" a man called from the vestibule.

The doors opened, light flooding the room as two uninformed officers stepped across the threshold. Guns drawn, bodies stiff with tension, they gestured for Henry to step away from the cuffed man.

"Everyone on the ground. Hands where we can see them."

"I'm cuffed. These jokers cuffed me," the perp yelled, but he dropped to his knees and then his stomach.

He knew the drill.

Henry did, too.

His ID was in his pocket, and within minutes he was free to stand up and move around.

Tessa was sitting a few feet away, her face pale, a smudge of blood on her neck. Dwarfed in Henry's coat, she looked small and very much alone.

He pulled her to her feet, tugged her into his arms.

She rested her forehead against his chest, her body stiff. "I am so sorry, Henry," she said.

"For what?"

"Bringing this here."

"You didn't. Patrick did."

"That's an easy out, and I'm not going to take it. I should have gone to the police before I left Napa Valley. I should have pressed charges. I should have—"

"Don't," he said, because he'd heard the same kind of comments dozens of times from dozens of victims who'd believed that they could have somehow changed the course of things.

"What?" She stepped back. "Tell the truth?"

"You are not to blame for what happened to you."

"I'm not concerned about what happened to me. I'm concerned about everyone else whose lives have been turned upside down because of choices I've made." She glanced at the hand-cuffed man. "I really need to get some air."

She stepped past Henry, ignoring an officer who told her to wait.

Henry followed, walking through the vestibule and into the icy rain. Chief Simpson was striding across the lot, and Tessa pivoted in the other direction.

"Everything okay?" the chief asked, his rain gear slick with moisture.

"That depends on who you ask."

"I'd ask Tessa, but she doesn't look like she's in the mood for talking."

"The guy we just apprehended claims her ex sent him here."

"I've made some calls. Patrick Hamilton has been out of the country on a buying trip for the past month. He traveled to China, and now he's in Thailand."

"Who'd you hear that from?" Henry asked, his attention still on Tessa. She'd reached the edge of the lot and was stepping into the icy field that led to the cemetery.

"His wife. She faxed me copies of the tickets and his visa. I checked with the airport. He was on the plane four weeks ago."

"Long-distance calls are pretty cheap nowadays. He could have arranged all of this without stepping foot back in the country."

"He could have, and maybe he did, but that's something we have to prove. Right now, all I have are a few fingerprints we pulled from Tessa's place. We already ran them through the system and got a hit. Justin Carter. Felony arrest in California two years ago for robbery. No weapon involved, and the judge let him off with probation. I've asked the California state police to see if they can track him down."

"I have a feeling they're not going to need to," Henry said. "We've probably got him cuffed in the church."

"That would sure make my life easier." Chief

Simpson shifted his attention to Tessa. She was still picking her way across the field. "We'll need to get her testimony eventually, but we've processed her house. Maybe you should bring her back home. Let her get some rest. She's been through a lot these past few weeks. Your associate is inside, right? She witnessed what went down in the church?"

"Yes."

"I'll get her statement and then give her a lift back to your in-laws' place. I wanted to stop by there and check on the Banning kid anyway."

"Has his father decided to talk?"

"He still has his lips sealed tighter than the doors of Fort Knox. We tried to trace the number the photos were texted to, but the phone was prepaid. Interesting thing, though—money was transferred into his bank account last night. Eight-hundred dollars."

"From?"

"An offshore account. No way to trace it. Like the phone, it's a dead-end."

"That's not much of a price for spending the rest of your life in jail." But, maybe for Tom, it was enough.

"No, but it would pay for a couple months of medication for Mrs. Banning," the chief responded. "Unfortunately, she doesn't have access to the account. It's in Tom's name. There's another account that she's co-listed on. Three dollars and fifty-two cents in that one."

"Great guy," Henry muttered.

"My thoughts exactly. The church is gathering a special offering to help offset some of her medical costs. And, some of the local businesses are offering food and services to the Bannings for free. The world isn't as dark a place as people like Tom make it appear to be. You'd better catch Tessa before she walks herself right into the Atlantic Ocean."

Henry followed Tessa's path across the parking lot and into the field. She'd made it into the oldest section of the cemetery and was walking on a narrow dirt path, her hands shoved in the pockets of his coat, her ponytail crooked, tendrils of hair clinging to her nape and her shoulders.

"Tessa!" he called, not wanting to startle her.

She stopped but didn't turn to look at him.

"It's not the best night for a leisurely stroll," he said as he reached her side.

"I've always liked snow," she replied.

"It's more ice than snow tonight."

"I'm still going to enjoy it." She raised her face to the sky, and he could see that she was crying.

"He's not worth your tears, Tessa."

"I'm not crying about him." She didn't wipe

away the tears, and she didn't lower her face. She let snow, ice and tears slide down her cheeks and drip down into the hollow of her throat.

"Then what are the tears for?" They reached a small gazebo that had been erected decades ago, its white cupola a shelter for weary wanderers. Tiny fairy lights had been strung from the eaves, and they flickered as the wind blew through.

"I love this place," Tessa said, ignoring the question as she walked into the gazebo and sat on a bench. "During the day, you can see the bay from here."

"And at night, when the sky is clear, you can see a million stars dancing over the ocean. Or that's what Aria tells me. The girls and I have spent a lot of time here. Sometimes, in the summer, we stay and watch the fireflies."

"Is Diane buried in the cemetery?"

"Yes. Provincetown was her favorite place. It seemed like what she'd want."

"I'm sorry, Henry. I know you were looking forward to sharing a lifetime with her," she said.

"We shared *her* lifetime. It's taken me a lot of years, but I've realized that is enough."

"Enough for what?" she asked, scuffing the toe of her foot against the floorboards. If she was still crying, he couldn't tell. Melted snow and ice were dripping from her hair and sliding down her face.

"Enough to be happy with." He brushed moisture from her cheeks, her skin cold against his warm palms. "Tell me why you were crying."

"I spent nine years living in a graveyard of dead dreams, pretending it was Cinderella's castle. If that's not sad enough to cry over, I don't know what is."

"You were young—"

"I don't want platitudes, Henry. I want to plant flowers in the wreckage of my old life, and then I want to watch them bloom."

"So, plant them," he said, his hands slipping from her cheeks to her shoulders.

"It's not that easy."

"It's as easy as you allow it to be," he responded, studying her face and seeing the fearful girl she'd been and the determined woman she'd become.

He touched the scar near her temple, his fingers drifting over the narrow white line. "You're stronger than you think you are, Tessa."

"I know I'm strong, but I'm also really tired." She bit her lower lip, her gaze shifting away, and he wondered if she was thinking about sleepless nights filled with terror and long days spent trying to avoid the inevitable abuse. Or, if she was thinking about more recent events and wondering if her life would ever really be her own.

"Tomorrow will be a better day," he said.

"Another platitude?" She stood, and he did the same, touching her waist when she would have walked away.

"Would you rather have a truth?"

"Always."

"Maybe it won't be better, but you're going to face it down just like you did this one and the one before it. And, if all you can do is keep facing your troubles head-on one day at a time, that's what you'll do. Until, one day, you look back and you can't believe how far you've come."

"*One day* seems like a long way away," she said, but there was a smile at the corners of her mouth and the hint of one in her eyes.

"Just finish today before you worry about that." He touched the thin scar near her temple, tracing it to her ear. He should have stopped there. It would have been the wise thing to do.

But he traced a line from her ear to her mouth, touching the tiny curve at the corner of it. He bent his head and kissed the spot, tasting the smile on her lips.

It didn't seem like enough.

He pulled her closer, his fingers splayed across her back as he kissed her again.

The world stood still, the rain and snow hung suspended in the sky and everything Henry thought he knew about himself shifted.

Because he'd never expected to fall in love again.

Diane had been his first love, and he'd planned for her to be his last.

But he was falling for Tessa, losing himself to her courage, her strength, her determination. His heart had known that long before he'd kissed her.

He pulled back, looked into her face. "Tessa—"

"What was that for?" she asked, her fingers pressed to her lips as if she could feel the heat of his kiss there.

"You. Me. Us."

"There is no us."

"There could be."

"For how long? A few weeks? A month? Will we last until spring arrives and someone better comes along?" Her voice was shaking, her hands fisted, and he realized he'd made a mistake. He'd moved too fast, given her the impression that her beauty was all he was interested in.

"If you think any of those things, you don't know me very well," he said calmly, stepping back to give her some space. Fairy lights were shimmering in her hair, and moisture was sliding down her cheeks. This time, he knew it was from her tears.

"What else is there, Henry, besides a few months of fun? A guy like you doesn't spend forever with a woman like me," she replied. Despite the tears, her eyes were cold, her expression hard.

"Exactly what kind of guy am I? And what kind of woman are you?" he asked.

"You're a professional. You make good money. You have a nice future ahead of you and two beautiful little girls who need to have good influences in their lives. Not bad ones."

"If you're implying that you're a bad influence and shouldn't be around the girls, then I think we need to spend some time talking about what being a bad influence actually means."

"I'm not implying anything. I'm stating that you and I come from different worlds."

"And?"

"It's probably best if we stay in them."

"If that's the best excuse you can come up with for keeping your distance, it's not a very good one." He sounded cold. He felt cold. He was a lot of things, but he wasn't judgmental.

"It's not an excuse for anything."

"Right," he muttered "And I'm not the father of two girls."

"You don't understand, Henry."

"Then explain it so I do."

"I'm trying to make this easy on both of us," she said.

"Make *what* easy? Because, from where I'm standing, our relationship was plenty easy. Until you decided to complicate it."

"See? That's what I mean. You're talking about a relationship. I don't want one."

"There are all kinds of relationships, Tessa," he said, biting out each word. "Which kinds do you not want?"

She pressed her lips together, and he knew what she'd almost said—that she didn't want any relationships. That she'd been happy and content to be on her own, living a solitary existence in her little college."

"I didn't take you for a coward," he muttered, angry because he wasn't going to force himself into her life, he wasn't going to demand what she wasn't willing to give.

But he didn't want to walk away from her.

She stared into his eyes, but she didn't speak, and when he'd given her enough time to say something that would change things, he scowled. "If you're ready to go home, I'll drive you there."

"I just don't want to hurt you," she said quietly.

"No. You don't want to be hurt." He turned on his heel and walked away.

She followed silently.

When they reached the SUV, he held her door while she climbed in, but he didn't bother speaking. He'd said everything he could.

The rest was up to her.

# ELEVEN

The thing about loneliness was that it hurt if you let it. In the years since she'd left Napa Valley, Tessa had worked hard not to let it. She'd taught herself to enjoy silence, to revel in walking into the empty cottage, and to find comfort in her own company.

Things had been going great until she'd met Henry and his family.

Now she dreaded the hours after work. Returning home after her evening class was even worse. She'd finally taken the makeup exam she'd been studying for, and despite all the distractions, she felt like it had gone well.

There was no one to share the news with.

Class ended at ten. The drive back to her place took nearly an hour and a half. By the time she pulled up to the cottage, everyone she knew whom she could share with was asleep.

And the one person she wanted to share with had left Provincetown the previous day.

She frowned.

She shouldn't be so tempted to call Henry.

She also shouldn't have checked her phone sixteen times to see if *he'd* contacted *her*.

She'd made it clear that she'd wanted nothing from him. She had played it safe, because that had made more sense than taking a chance on something as inconsequential as a romantic relationship.

But she hadn't been able to forget the taste of his lips, the gentleness of his touch or the heartache she'd felt when he'd turned and walked away.

Without even realizing it was happening, Henry had taken up residence in her heart.

She'd been too cowardly to let him stay there.

Three nights after telling him they should keep their lives separate, she was still trying to convince herself she'd done the right thing.

He deserved someone better than her, someone who didn't have baggage filled with the deadweight of her abusive relationship.

But she missed hearing his voice, seeing his smile and watching as he interacted with the girls.

According to Chief Simpson, Henry and Jessica had returned to Boston on Sunday afternoon. Aside from the kidnapping, the crimes perpetrated against Tessa were the jurisdiction of local law officials. The Provincetown police were conducting the investigation, but the FBI was still willing to help if it was necessary. Chief Simpson had made it very clear to Tessa that he didn't think it was. He was working with the state police, the California Highway Patrol and the Thai military police to try to locate Patrick. Sheila had been cooperating, but she hadn't heard from her husband in nearly a week, and she had no idea what part of Thailand he was in.

Chief Simpson suspected he'd gotten wind of what was happening in the States and was keeping a low profile. He also suspected that Patrick might never resurface. He'd had plenty of money when he'd left the United States. He'd been the sole beneficiary of Ryan's interest in the antiques stores, and he'd liquidated nearly a million dollars' worth of inventory before he'd left the country. None of that money had appeared in the business accounts. The police believed Patrick had syphoned it into offshore accounts, and that when he'd booked his trip overseas, he'd had no intention of returning.

Tessa hoped that was the case.

The farther away he stayed, the safer she'd feel.

She shivered as she pulled up to the cottage. She'd left the porch light on, and she could see the living-room light behind the curtains in the front windows. The cottage looked the same as it did every time she returned to it. Usually, she felt elated to be walking into her own place. Since Friday evening, she'd felt nothing but tired.

She grabbed her backpack from the passenger seat and walked across the yard, her keys in hand, a hard knot in her stomach.

She'd wanted so much more than this.

She'd wanted all the little things that other people often took for granted—kids running to greet her when she opened the door, dishes in the kitchen sink, pets creating chaos, the television turned on, lights left burning when no one was in the room. She'd wanted broken dishes and Lego on the floor and piles of laundry waiting to be washed or folded. She'd wanted a messy life with messy people who laughed too loudly and sang off-key.

More than anything, she'd just wanted to love and to be loved. She had wanted to look into someone else's heart and know she would always have a home there.

She shoved her keys in the doorknob and unlocked it, stepping inside and dropping her backpack on the floor.

Her cell phone rang, and she grabbed it, her heart leaping as she checked to see if it was

Henry. Every day for three days, she'd hoped he'd call. Every day, he hadn't.

She could have called him. She knew that.

She *should* have.

But she was terrified of being vulnerable. Even with someone as trustworthy as Henry.

It was a local number, and she answered quickly, thinking it might be someone from the police department giving her an update on the case.

"Hello?"

"Tessa?" a little girl said.

"Aria?" she asked, glancing at the number again. She had Rachelle and Brett's cell phone numbers. She had their home number, too. This wasn't any of those.

"I did something really bad," she whispered.

"You never do anything bad, honey," Tessa responded.

"This time, I did. And I'm really sorry. I really am." She was obviously crying, and Tessa's heart broke for her.

"Where's your daddy, sweetheart?" she asked.

"He had to work on a big case."

"What about your Nana or Pop-pop?"

"Watching television, so they don't know I'm gone."

"Gone?" Tessa went cold at the word, a dozen

scenarios filling her head. None of them good. "What do you mean 'gone'?"

"We were coming to see you. He promised, because I missed you."

"You and Everly?"

"No, me and the man who was cleaning school today."

"What man?" But she knew.

Of course, she knew.

Patrick didn't like to lose.

"He was cleaning the school, and me and Everly saw him in the hall when we were going to the bathroom. He said we looked sad, and I told him that was because I really missed you, and he said he knew you, and he even knew that you have a scar and where you live and everything."

"You're not with him, are you, Aria?" She tried to keep her voice calm, but she knew panic was seeping through. She managed to put the call on speaker and find Henry's number.

She shot him a text, her fingers trembling, her heart pulsing in her ears.

"Aria?" she prodded.

"Guess again," Patrick said, his voice as silky and dry as a viper's hiss.

"What do you want, Patrick?" she asked, praying that Henry would respond to her text.

"You know what I want."

"The watch is evidence in the investigation against you. The police have it."

"I don't need a watch, you little idiot. I have more than enough money to keep me floating for a very long time."

"Then, what?"

"You. Me. Back the way it used to be." He chuckled.

"You're married."

"And?"

"I'm sure Sheila won't want to share you with someone else," she said as she stared at the phone and willed Henry to respond.

"Sheila was a means to an end."

"What end?"

"The two of us flying off to another country and living happily-ever-after. It takes money to do that, babe, and Sheila had millions of dollars of life insurance on my dearly departed business partner."

"You don't want me, Patrick. You never did."

"Men always want what they don't have. I was bored with you for a while, but I'm ready to pick up where we left off."

"You're lying." She raced to the landline and dialed 911, praying he wouldn't be able to hear the operator. She didn't dare speak or ask for help. She set the receiver on the kitchen counter and walked to the mudroom doorway, hoping her side of the conversation would reach the operator's ears.

"Maybe, but what does that matter? I've got the kid. You want her. We'll do an exchange."

"I already told you, I don't have the watch."

"I don't need the watch. The police already have that idiot Justin in custody. They've got the guy he hired, too."

"Tom Banning?"

"I don't ask names. I just ask if jobs are done."

"What job?"

"I wanted the watch. Aside from Justin it was the only thing linking me to Ryan's murder. Justin needed a distraction so that he could get in your place and look for it."

"You had someone nearly burn down a diner because you needed a distraction?" she asked.

"*I* didn't need it. Justin said it would make his job easier. I needed Justin. At least until the job was done. So, I did what needed to be done to keep him happy."

"You just sat back and watched the show, huh?"

"We were together for nine years, and you never figured out that I don't like to get my hands dirty?" he said, chuckling.

"You're insane."

"I'm smart. I know what I want. I go after it. I don't let people get in my way, and I don't leave loose ends. Poor Justin is going to meet a painful end while he's waiting for trial, and his bozo Banning is going to, as well. Of course, all that will happen after I'm out of reach of the authorities."

"I was told you were in Thailand. If you'd stayed there, you wouldn't have anything to worry about."

"Money buys a lot of things. Even a look-alike to take your identification and hop on a plane to another country. You know that. You purchased an entirely new life with what you stole from me. Right, *Tessa*?"

"I didn't use any of your money or antiques to fund my new life. I pawned my jewelry."

"That jewelry was mine. You were mine. Everything we had together was *mine*!" he roared, and she thought she heard Aria sobbing in the background.

"What do you want, Patrick?" she said. "Tell me straight-up, because I'm not as smart as you, and I can't be expected to figure it out."

"Stop with the false humility, baby. We both know you are plenty smart. That was the problem. You should have been a pretty face and an empty head," he said, his voice dripping with sarcasm and hatred.

"What do you want?" she repeated.

"A fair exchange. You for the kid."

"Okay."

"Just like that? You're not going to ask what I plan to do once I have you?"

"Me for Aria, but I'm not going anywhere with you until I'm certain she's safe."

"You will do exactly what I say, or you'll both die."

"Then, how about you start talking and say something that matters? Because, I would like to get this over with," she responded, knowing her flip tone would annoy him. She wanted to keep him talking. She wanted the 911 operator to hear as much as possible.

"You'd better keep that smart mouth in check. I don't make it a habit of killing kids, but I'll make an exception this time, if I have to."

"I didn't realize you made it a habit of killing," she said, opening a drawer and grabbing a paring knife. She tucked it into her boot.

"You should have asked more questions when we were dating. My parents died in an unfortunate accident when I was eighteen. My grandfather died a few months later. And I inherited everything."

"You killed them?"

"I prefer to say that I sent them off on their final adventure before they were ready. Now, how about you stop wasting my time, and we get down to business. I'll be at Pilgrim Monument in an hour. I suggest you arrive before me."

"I'll be there."

"No car. It's only five miles from your place. An easy walk. No cell phone, either. You bring either of those things, and your boyfriend won't ever see his daughter again. If the police show up, same thing. Come alone. And in case your insipid little brain doesn't understand what that means, I don't want anyone with you. Not your boss. Not your neighbor. Not even your best friend's puppy."

"All right."

"Of course it is," he crooned. "You know, I've really missed how agreeable you learned to be. Maybe we can get back to that. Eventually."

He disconnected, and she hurried to the landline and lifted it. The call had disconnected.

Or, maybe, it had never gone through.

She thought about calling again, but she was afraid the police would head to the monument, lights and sirens blaring.

If Aria died, she'd never forgive herself.

She called Henry, and when he didn't pick up, she left a brief message. She didn't have time for more than that. The monument was a forty-minute walk from the house.

She was certain Patrick knew that.

If she didn't hurry, she'd be late.

He had always hated when people were late.

And he had always loved setting her up to fail.

He'd loved to watch her struggle, and he'd loved meting out punishments.

This time, though, she wouldn't fail.

She couldn't.

Aria's life depended on that.

He was driving too fast. Henry knew it, but he couldn't make himself ease off the accelerator.

They were ten minutes away from the monument.

Tessa's message had been left thirty minutes ago.

He'd tried to return her call, but he'd reached her voice mail. He'd retried a half-dozen times since then, franticly, desperately.

Aria was gone.

And he wouldn't even know that if Tessa hadn't told him.

He'd been tying up some loose ends on a case he was closing, immersing himself in work because that was easier than being at home, fielding questions about why the girls couldn't call their best friend, Tessa. Why they hadn't been able to see her on the weekend. When they would be able to visit her again.

He hadn't had the heart to tell them that they wouldn't be seeing her, that he planned to stay as far away from the Cape as possible for a while. Not because he didn't care about Tessa, but because he cared too much.

He wanted her to be happy.

Whether that meant alone or with him.

The girls were too young to understand that, and they were too young to not get attached to a woman who showered them with affection and attention.

He had always understood the hole Diane had left in his life and in the lives of her parents, but he hadn't realized how much of a hole she'd left in the twins' lives until Tessa had begun to fill it.

He didn't want them to be hurt.

He didn't want Tessa to be hurt.

Time seemed like the best solution to a problem he wasn't sure how to fix, but while he'd been working late at the office, Aria had snuck out of Brett and Rachelle's Boston townhome. She'd left a note on her pillow, sworn her sister to secrecy and climbed out a lower-level window to meet a man who'd promised to take her to visit Tessa.

He'd warned the girls about strangers.

He'd told them to never go off with one.

But according to Everly, the man wasn't a stranger. He was a janitor at school. One who'd known everything about Tessa, who'd described her house, Provincetown and even the church they attended. He'd told the girls that he could take them to visit Tessa, but it had to be a secret, because otherwise their grandparents would ruin things.

He'd given them a time, told them to climb out a window and sneak to his car. He'd even promised to bring everyone for dinner once they'd reached Provincetown.

Everly had been eager to go along with the plan until the last minute. She'd helped Aria remove a screen from a living-room window, and then she'd chickened out.

At least, that's how she'd described it to Henry.

It had been Aria, his timid child, who'd followed through.

And now she was gone, kidnapped by a man who'd had his business partner killed for profit.

"You should probably slow down," Jessica said calmly as he sped away from the Provincetown Municipal Airport. Thanks to Wren's connections, they'd been able to fly in on a chartered jet, the twenty-minute flight from Boston seeming to last an eternity.

"You probably should," Wren agreed. "We rented a car so that Patrick wouldn't recognize the vehicle. If you're flying along the road in a rented vehicle, he might get suspicious."

She was right.

He forced himself to slow down. He could see the monument in the distance, glowing white against the clear black sky. "Have you tried Tessa again?" he asked.

"Only five times since we disembarked from the plane. My calls are going straight to voice mail."

"Chief Simpson?"

"He and a team of his officers are meeting us on the corner of Winslow and Mayflower. They're on foot, but he says he thinks they got into position before Patrick arrived."

"Is Patrick there?"

"They have an officer in an unmarked car across from the monument. Tessa walked past him three minutes ago, but he hasn't spotted Patrick or Aria."

"If he hurt her…" He stopped. Threats were useless, and retaliating wouldn't bring back Aria if Patrick had killed her. Just the thought filled him with cold dread and overwhelming sorrow.

"He didn't," Jessica said. "He's too into the game. He wants to keep his bargaining chip, so he can keep playing for a while longer."

"I hope you're right."

"I am. Patrick is a typical narcissist. He loves watching people squirm, and he gets a thrill out of winning at whatever game he's playing. To him, people are simply a means to an end. Aria isn't his target, and unless something goes very wrong, he's probably not going to hurt her."

"It's the 'probably' part of that statement that I'm not much liking."

"I'm giving you all the information, Henry, but I don't think we're going to have to worry about anything going wrong. Tessa handled this well. She contacted you, and she's doing what he's asked. Her goal is the same as ours—make sure Aria stays safe."

"My goal is to make certain they both stay safe."

"Once we get Aria out of harm's way, we'll work in extracting Tessa," Wren said, her phone ringing.

She answered, her tone terse. "Agent Santino. Yes. Okay. We're a minute out."

She slid the phone into her pocket. "Patrick has been spotted. He parked at a theater near the monument and got out of his car. Aria is with him. From what the officer said, she looks fine."

"Let's make sure she stays that way," he said grimly, turning onto Winslow. Pilgrim was just ahead, and he slowed as he neared it, afraid Patrick might notice a car at his time of the night in this part of town.

He didn't see any sign of the chief or his officers.

Good.

If Henry couldn't see them, Patrick couldn't, either.

He parked in front of a small ranch-style house, turned off the engine of the rental car and jumped out.

He'd have run toward the monument, if Wren hadn't grabbed his arm and yanked him back.

"You've always been cool-headed in a crisis, Henry. How about we don't change that tonight?"

She was right.

Panicking wasn't going to save his daughter.

It wasn't going to save Tessa.

Patrick was a coldhearted murderer, but Henry was part of a team that new exactly how to stop men like him.

He nodded, his gaze drawn to a small group of people that stepped out from behind a house. Simpson. Kayla. Three other uniformed officers. They were moving with confidence. Hurrying but not frantic.

Tessa had called 911 from her landline while she was on the phone with Patrick. The call had been recorded, the details had been handed over to the police department. They'd been in place and ready for a half hour.

Henry needed to trust them, trust his team, trust God.

He needed to believe that evil could be defeated, that good could prevail, that everything he worked for, that he valued, that he lauded as worthwhile, was exactly what would get his daughter and Tessa out of this alive.

And then he needed to stop panicking and do whatever he had to, to make sure that happened.

# TWELVE

It was twenty-nine degrees, but Tessa was covered in a layer of drying sweat, her heart still pounding frantically as she circled the monument for what seemed like the hundredth time.

She'd made the forty-minute walk in less than thirty-five. She'd still expected Patrick to be waiting when she arrived. Instead, the parking area was empty, light glowing off the granite facade of the giant monolith.

She had spent time at the monument before. She'd walked to the top and admired the view. She'd read the plaque. She'd visited the museum. She'd done all the things that a tourist would.

She'd never thought of the place as eerie, but it felt that way now. She skirted around the side of the tower, eyeing the dark corners of the parking lot. A small hill led down to the sidewalk, and she thought about going there, but she was afraid Patrick would arrive, not see her and drive away with Aria.

She glanced at her watch. It had been nearly an hour since he'd contacted her. Had he changed his mind? Changed the plan? Was he calling her cell phone trying to give her other instructions?

She'd left that at home. Just like he'd told her to.

But Patrick had always loved stacking the cards against her.

Without her phone, she had no way of calling for help and no way of knowing if anyone was trying to reach her. The person she most wanted to hear from was Henry. She wanted to know that he'd gotten her message and that help was on the way.

It certainly wasn't coming from the local police. She hadn't heard sirens. She hadn't seen any police cruisers. Either her 911 call hadn't gone through, or the operator had thought it was a joke.

One way or another, she was on her own.

"Not on your own," she muttered. "God is with you, and He's not going to let Patrick win."

"He has so far," Patrick said, stepping out from the dark entrance of the monument.

Her heart jumped, her pulse raced, but she wasn't going to let him know how terrified she was. He lived off the fear of others. He thrived when he knew he had control.

"How long have you been there?" she asked,

forcing a calmness to her voice that she didn't feel. She didn't see Aria, but she didn't dare ask about the little girl. Not right away. If she did, he'd make certain to keep the information from her for as long as he could.

"Three laps' worth. We enjoyed watching you getting more and more worried that I wasn't going to show. Didn't we, kid?" he asked, reaching into the dark alcove and pulling Aria from the shadows.

Tessa's knees went weak with relief, but when Aria tried to run to her, she shook her head.

"That's right. Stay with me, kiddo," Patrick laughed. "We get to be best friends until I decide what I'm going to do with you." He yanked her closer, and she stumbled, her hair falling in a tangled mess of black curls around her face.

She'd been crying. Tessa could see the tearstains on her face. "It's going to be okay, Aria."

"No. It isn't," Patrick replied. "Your good buddy messed with the wrong person, and now someone has to pay. The question is, will it be you, or will it be her?"

"Tessa, run away!" Aria yelled.

Patrick laughed again. "She's not going to run. She's much too nice to leave a little munchkin like you with a man like me."

"Let her go, Patrick."

"I don't think so."

"You said you would."

"I also said I was going to marry you after you moved in with me. Did that happen?"

She didn't answer.

"Did it?" he shouted.

In another lifetime, she'd have cowered away from his rage.

But she'd grown a lot since she'd run from him. She'd learned a lot about herself and about what she was capable of.

"If you'd been a decent kind of human being, it would have. But you weren't. So, no."

"You've gotten really mouthy since you left, haven't you?" he spat, his eyes blazing. "But you're not going to be mouthy when I'm up at the top of this tower, holding this little brat over the edge. Then you're going to be begging for forgiveness."

He dragged Aria back into the monument, ignoring the little girl's flailing fists and kicking feet.

Tessa raced after them, desperate to free Aria from his grip and give her a chance to run.

"I'll beg you now, Patrick. If that's what you want," she said as she darted under the granite arch and realized he'd picked the lock that opened the gates there.

He whirled around, his face hidden by darkness. "Fine. Beg."

She dropped to her knees, and she could see his smile through the darkness.

"Please, Tessa!" Aria cried, her sobs echoing through the structure. "Will you go get my daddy? He'll save us."

"If he were going to save you, he'd have done it by now. Your father is garbage. Just like every police officer," Patrick said coldly.

"He's not garbage!" Aria wiped her hand across her cheeks, swiping at the tears.

"You're a kid. I guess I can forgive you for your wrong opinions. Now, shut up. I'm waiting for your buddy to beg me to forgive her for all the trouble she's caused. Go ahead. Beg."

"I'm sorry, Patrick," she said. "I should never have left you."

"Are you kidding?" he crowed. "Your leaving me was the best thing that had happened to me in a long time. Out you went. In Sheila came. A nice little revolving door of women, and I didn't even have to kill you to make it happen."

"Sheila is too good for you," she said, trying to get to the paring knife without him noticing.

"She's certainly a step up from you," he responded.

When she didn't argue, he sighed. "The problem is, no one is really good enough for me. I've dated plenty of women, and all of them are fine for a while. Eventually, though, they all become bores. When I get bored, I spend money. Really, when you think about it, it's your fault Ryan had to die."

"Mine?"

"Sure. At first you were exciting. You had a lot of spunk, and I liked that. After a while, you became like every other woman I'd ever dated. A sniveling leech who was more interested in taking from me than giving to me what I was due. You know what that is?"

"Praise?" she guessed. "Adulation?"

"I like those things, but what I deserve is absolute devotion. No questions. No arguments. I thought if I dated someone young, I might be able to make that happen. But my effort was wasted on you. You ended up boring me, and I had to go spend money to make myself feel better. I got myself into some financial trouble at the shop, and Ryan found out. He wanted to have a rational discussion about the money that was missing from the accounts. Unfortunately, I did not."

"So, you killed him."

"I paid someone to kill him. I'm sure you remember that I don't like to get my hands dirty. Although, in your case, I might make an exception. You've put me through a lot of trouble. If you hadn't taken that watch—"

"I didn't realize what it meant. I had no idea it was Ryan's until after you came looking for it."

"Of course you didn't. I was never worried about you figuring it out. I was worried about you selling it and someone else figuring it out. There are a few people with brains in their heads. You're not one of them. You're stupid. Just like I always told you."

"She's not stupid!" Aria cried, and he laughed.

"Yes, she is, and you're a little spitfire." He paused. "Not that either of those things matter to me. Once I settle in Thailand, I'll go into business again, build even more of a fortune, find someone who understands the rules required of anyone who wants to be with me."

Tessa lunged, throwing her weight into his torso, the knife arching toward him.

"Run, Aria!" she shouted.

"You're going to regret that!" Patrick yelled, grabbing her wrist before the knife made contact, his fingers digging into bone.

She'd forgotten how strong he was, how quick.

Aria sprinted out from under the monument, her legs and arms churning as she ran, but Tessa was caught, her arm hiked up in a painful position, the knife dropping from her fingers.

"That," Patrick panted, "was stupid. And now you've made me angry. Just like you always do. Too bad. I was thinking about taking you to

Thailand, but I'm afraid I'm going to have to leave you here." He backhanded her, the explosive power of the blow sending her into the wall.

He had her by the hair before she could right herself, the knife pressed against her jugular.

She knew this waltz. She'd danced it with him before.

"Walk," he growled.

"Where?"

"Up." He shoved her toward the entrance that led to the top of the monument. "Maybe I'll change my mind about killing you before we get to the top."

Aria was screaming as she darted into the street, her hair flying around her face.

Henry snatched her up, dragging her behind the nearest parked car, avoiding the fists and feet she was using to try to fend him off.

"It's okay, honey," he murmured. "It's Daddy."

"Daddy?" She stopped fighting, her chest heaving as she looked at his face. She touched his cheek as if she wanted to be sure he was really who he claimed to be.

"Yes," he responded.

"I've been praying and praying that you would come find us. That bad man has Tessa, and it's all my fault."

"It's his fault. Not yours, and I'm going to help

Tessa, but I need you to be brave and stay here with Officer Kayla, okay?"

She nodded, brushing thick strands of hair from her cheeks and looking him square in the eyes. "Tessa saved my life. Now you need to save hers."

He nodded, kissed her forehead and handed her to Kayla.

Wren was a few feet away, watching the tower through binoculars. "They're heading up. I just saw a shadow go past the first window."

"The gates into the monument are locked this time of year," Chief Simpson muttered. "He shouldn't be doing anything other than bringing her this way."

That's what they'd planned for. He'd head back to his car with Tessa and Aria. They'd swoop in and stop him from leaving.

But life didn't often work out according to plan, and Henry wasn't going to wait around hoping that Patrick would eventually appear. "I'm going inside," he said.

"If he has a gun, he'll have a clear shot down. It's a spiral up, straight drop down to the center," the chief explained.

Henry nodded. He'd looked at photos on his way in on the plane. "I'll try not to let him shoot me."

"This isn't a joke, Henry," Wren cautioned.

"He's already killed once. He's not going to hesitate to kill again."

"That's what I'm worried about. Every second we waste trying to come up with a new plan is another few steps between us and the person we're trying to save."

Wren frowned. "You're right."

"There's some scrub on the other side of the monument that might provide cover on the way in," Chief Simpson suggested. "How many people do you want going in?"

"Me, my two agents and you. Should be fine." Wren motioned for Jessica to fall in beside them.

"Let's go, then," the chief said, moving between parked vehicles and sticking to the shadows as they left, heading perpendicular to the monument. When they were a dozen yards away, he cut in toward it, heading up a hill through thick scrub.

They stayed low, following the curved granite wall until they reached one of the rectangular doorways that opened to the interior of the monument.

There was a gate just beyond it, yawning open.

The chief gestured for them to follow him through another doorway that led up a narrow passageway.

Henry could hear footsteps, and he looked up,

catching a quick glimpse of a shadow moving fifty feet above them.

Wren touched his arm, gestured for him to take the lead.

He went willingly, moving as quickly and as silently as he could up the stairs and ramps that separated him from Tessa.

Something fell on the stairway above him, the sound echoing through the chamber. He thought he heard Tessa gasp, but he couldn't be certain.

He'd let things go too long after their last conversation. He realized that now.

He'd wanted to give her space and a chance to figure out how much of her heart she was willing to risk to be in a relationship with him.

More than that, he'd wanted her to trust him. He'd wanted her to know that he was a safe place to land.

And he'd wanted her to realize that without any coercion or convincing from him.

If he was honest with himself, he could admit that he'd been hurt, that he'd been just as eager to avoid repeating that as he'd accused Tessa of being.

He'd been a fool.

He wanted the opportunity to tell her that.

He prayed he'd have the opportunity.

It was a long way up to the top of the tower.

A lot of things could go wrong before any of them reached it.

*Please, Lord, protect Tessa*, he prayed silently as he continued upward.

The sound of another scuffle broke the quiet, and something bounced off the railing above him. It struck the granite block wall and fell to the ground, thirty-feet below.

A man cursed and feet pounded along a ramp somewhere above Henry. He thought, at first, that someone was racing up the stairs, but the sound seemed to be getting louder.

He glanced up, saw a pale figure sprinting down from the highest section of the tower.

Tessa!

And Patrick was right behind her!

# THIRTEEN

In her nightmares, Tessa always ran from Patrick. Through towns. Through buildings. Through churches. She would run as far and as fast as she could, but she never managed to escape. No matter which direction she went, he was always there. Blocking her path. Keeping her from safety. She'd wake in a cold sweat, her body numb with fear, her mind slow to convince her that she was okay, that it was only a dream.

She wished she could do that now—wake bathed in sweat, terrified but safe.

But this wasn't a dream.

She wasn't okay.

She was wide-awake, sprinting through Pilgrim Monument, Patrick right behind her, his nose bloody, his eyes blazing with fury.

"I. Will. Kill. You!" he roared, grabbing the back of her coat and throwing her against the railing.

She bucked against him, her back bowed, her

feet slipping. He thrust her back, his hand over her face as he tried to force her head over the side of the railing. Force *her* over.

How high were they? Seventy feet? A hundred?

Would it matter once she fell?

*Please, Lord*, she prayed. *Help me.*

"I should have killed you nine years ago, you little witch!" he screamed, spittle spraying her neck and chin.

She gagged, a dozen memories filling her head.

A hundred million moments of feeling helpless, alone and terrified trying to steal her will to fight.

But she was older now. Wiser. She'd learned what she could do if she was brave enough.

And she wasn't going to let him take that from her.

She smashed her foot into his instep, and he howled, his hand slipping from her face to her throat.

"Stupid little idiot," he yelled, his hot breath fanning her cheek as he pressed his weight into her and tried to lift her over the side railing.

She had her hands free, and she slammed one into his throat, knocking him back just enough for her to slip out from beneath him.

She tried to dart past, but he gave her a two-handed shove that sent her sprawling, her shoulder crashing into the edge of a stair.

She jumped up, pivoting away, and raced back in the direction she'd come. Up. Passing one window and another. She could hear him behind her, moving slowly and steadily. No rush. No hurry now. Whistling a cheerful tune that echoed in the cavernous space and settled deep into her bones.

She knew the tune.

She knew what it meant.

Patrick was happy.

He was getting what he wanted.

And what he wanted was Tessa at the top of the tower.

She slowed her pace, conserving her energy for the fight she knew was coming. He'd been enraged when she'd knocked the knife from his hand. When she'd flat-palmed him in the nose, she'd known he would kill her.

She'd thought she could outrun him, but rage seemed to have given him superhuman speed.

Now she was right back where she'd started the fight, a window near her shoulder looking out toward Cape Cod Bay. Starlight twinkled in the blue-black sky, the moon a yellow crescent high above.

She wanted a thousand more nights to enjoy the beauty of God's creation.

And she wanted just one more opportunity to make things right with Henry.

She'd been a fool to let him walk away.

She'd been terrified of losing her heart, and even more scared of losing herself. Of giving up the freedom she'd fought so hard for and finding herself in shackles again.

She'd hurt Henry with her doubt. She'd hurt the girls.

She'd let her fear control her the way Patrick once had, and she refused to do it again. She could hear him approaching, his feet purposely heavy on the nearest ramp, his song graciously cheerful.

"You might as well quit," he said as he finally reached her. "You can't win."

Maybe he was right.

Maybe she couldn't win.

But she *could* fight.

She waited until he was nearly an arm length away, and then she rammed him, the force of the attack throwing him backward. He fell down the ramp and came up swinging, his fist catching her in the side of the face.

She crashed to the floor, and he was on her, hands around her throat, strangling her the way he had so many times before.

She clawed at his hands, trying to get breath

into her desperate lungs, her vision going black, her arms going weak.

And then he was gone, and she could breathe again.

Henry cuffed Patrick and shoved him toward Wren.

"Good choice," she said.

"Was there another one?" he asked, his breath heaving from the race up the stairs.

"You could have tossed him over," Jessica responded, taking one of Patrick's arms and yanking him toward the ramp that led down. "It might have cost you your job, but it might have been worth it to get this scum off the planet."

"Shut up, you stupid little—" Patrick began.

"You have the right to remain silent, and you probably should," Jessica said, unfazed by the guy's bravado. "I'm taking him down. I'll have the local PD book him, but I'm assuming we plan to transport him to the field office for questioning?"

"Yes," Wren agreed, her gaze dropping to Tessa.

She was pale, bruises visible on her neck and her face.

"Are you okay?" Henry asked, kneeling beside her and lifting her wrist to take her pulse.

"I'm alive," she responded with a tired smile. "That's a lot better than the alternative. Aria—"

"Is fine. I left her with Kayla."

"How did she find you? I was worried sick when I told her to run. I had no idea if she'd be able to find help, and I was terrified of what might happen to her if she couldn't."

"We were just a few yards away. This place has been under surveillance since your nine-one-one call was received. Chief Simpson made the decision to keep things quiet. He didn't want to scare Patrick into doing something stupid."

"I was worried about that, too. I was afraid he'd hear sirens and realize I'd called for help. I wouldn't have been able to forgive myself if something had happened to Aria."

"She wasn't the only one that you needed to be worried about." He helped her to her feet, brushing hair from her cheeks. "I hope you know that Aria wasn't the only one on my mind when I rushed here from Boston. Now, how about we get out of here?"

"That sounds like a perfect plan. I've never been afraid of heights, but right now, I'd like to have my feet firmly planted on the ground."

"Do you think you can make it down on your own? Or do you want me to call an ambulance?"

"No ambulance. I don't have time. I've got—"

"Let me guess," he said. "A test you have to study for?"

"No." She shook her head, looking into his eyes. "A life I need to live."

"I don't suppose there's room in it for a few more people?" he asked, cupping her elbow as they walked down the ramp and onto a set of stairs.

"How many people are we talking about?" she asked, a smile at the corner of her lips.

"Five? Although, two of them are pint-size. Maybe we can count them as one."

Her smile fell away, and she stopped walking. "Henry—"

"I know you need some time, and I'm not trying to rush you into something you're not ready for, but—"

"I'm ready," she said, so quietly he almost didn't hear. "I was ready when you kissed me the other night—"

"I am not listening to this conversation," Wren called, and Tessa smiled.

"What I'm trying to say," she continued, "is that I don't want to let fear control my life. Not any longer. And when I'm with you, I feel braver than I have in a long time."

"That's not because of me, Tessa."

"It's because of *us*. Of how we are together. I realized that when I was at the top of the tower with Patrick. When I was with him, I felt diminished. When I'm with you, I don't. You make me want to be all the things I've dreamed of—strong and fearless and confident."

"You are all those things," he said, cupping her face and looking into her eyes.

"Maybe. Maybe I'm just learning to be. One way or another, if I'm going to fill my life with people, I want them to be people who challenge me to be my best self. That's what you do, Henry."

"Does that mean you have room for us?" he asked, his lips grazing hers.

"More than enough," she murmured against his lips.

He kissed her. Gently. Sweetly, because he wanted her to know how much he cherished her, and then he took her hand, and he led her out of the monument.

# EPILOGUE

The girls had flower crowns in their hair and white baskets in their hands, their gauzy dresses brushing the top of sparkly blue shoes. No heels. Although, they'd begged to be allowed the privilege.

Tessa would have conceded, but Henry had told them they could wear heels when they were old enough to walk in them without tripping. He didn't want any visits to the emergency room on their wedding day.

*Their* wedding day.

Even now, as she stood in a floor-length lace gown, facing the sanctuary doors and waiting for her cue to enter, she couldn't believe it was happening. After so many years of being alone, Henry had filled her life with everything good and wonderful and right.

One of the girls giggled, twirling around so that her dress whirled in a circle.

Everly. Of course. She'd spent the day coming up with excuses to call Tessa and check in. Just to make certain everything was going okay, she'd said. Tessa suspected she'd wanted to be sure the plans weren't changing, that they really were all going to walk down the aisle.

A sunset wedding had been a great idea. In theory.

The long day of waiting had been difficult on everyone.

Especially the twins.

"Everly Anne!" Rachelle chided. "You're going to wreck your beautiful hair."

"If she wrecks it, I can fix it," Aria said, clutching her flower basket as if her life depended on it.

She'd been quieter since she'd been tricked by Patrick. She hadn't been injured, but six months after the incident, she was more cautious than ever about strangers. She'd been worried about the wedding since the day Tessa and Henry had told the girls they planned to get married, often wondering aloud about the possibilities of bad guys being there.

Tessa and Henry had assured her that Patrick was in jail, and that he wouldn't ever be getting out, but Aria still seemed worried.

Tessa touched her shoulder, smiling when Aria met her eyes. "It's going to be okay, honey."

"There's going be a lot of people in there. If I see that guy, I'm going to yell, and you run, okay?"

"He won't be there, pumpkin. He's going to be in jail forever," she said, knowing that the pet name would make Aria smile.

"Why do you always call me pumpkin?"

"Because, pumpkin is one of my favorite things."

Aria grinned, but there was still fear in her eyes. They'd been taking her to a counselor, who'd been helping her work through her anxiety, but she was still often afraid.

Time.

Love.

That's what she needed.

Those things were healing balms to the troubled soul.

Tessa knew that. She'd lived it.

And, now she was here. In this place she'd never imagined she'd be. With people she cared about and who cared about her, looking into a future filled with possibility.

Soon, she'd be a registered nurse.

A mother to the twins.

A wife.

Her heart fluttered at the thought.

"You know what, Tessa?" Aria whispered.

"What?"

"You are beautiful."

"I guess most brides are," she said, smiling.

"You're not beautiful because you're a bride. You're beautiful because of the way you love us. And, the way you love Daddy. And, the way you fit into our lives. Just right."

"Thank you, honey," Tessa said, crouching so that they were face to face, her eyes burning with tears of joy and thankfulness. "You make it very easy for me to love you, and you give me a very comfortable place to fit."

"Are you crying?" Everly asked, twirling toward Tessa and stopping so close to Aria, the skirts of their dresses touched.

"Of course, she's not," Rachelle said, brushing a few strands of Everly's hair back into place. "This is a day for smiling and for laughing and for joy. Now, you two get yourselves ready. In just a minute, you'll be walking your new momma down the aisle," her voice broke.

Tessa straightened, taking Rachelle's hands and squeezing them gently.

"I know this must be bittersweet," she began, but Rachelle shook her head.

"There is nothing bitter about it. It's all sweet. Any tears that fall from these eyes are going to be joyous ones. The day we lost Diane, I prayed that God would bring something good out of the heartache. Over the years, He's shown me again and again that tragedy doesn't have to define my life. Today? He's showing me that lovely things can rise from the ashes of our brokenness. If we all allow them to."

Tessa smiled, but she couldn't speak past the lump in her throat.

This was what she'd always wanted—acceptance and family and home. What she'd hoped and longed and prayed for.

And, what she'd never really believed she would have. Until she'd met Henry.

The sanctuary doors opened, and Betty slipped into the vestibule, her eyes bright with excitement, her cheeks pink. She'd worn her best dress and low heels. Her hair was pulled away from her face with a tortoiseshell clip. If Hester had lived to see this day, the two of them would have been fast friends.

"Well, this it!" she proclaimed as she straightened Tessa's veil. "Are you ready?"

"Yes," Tessa responded, and Betty smiled.

"That's what I like to hear. Confidence!"

"We're confident, too, and we're ready," Everly said. "We've been ready for ages and ages and ages."

"I think she's right," Aria agreed, some of her somberness replaced by excitement. "I think we have been waiting an awfully long time."

"Well, girls, the wait is over. Hear that?" Betty asked as the organ music swelled into the first strains of the wedding march. "That's our cue. Now, each of you grab one of Tessa's hands, and let's go. We don't want to make your daddy wait. He might think you've all gone and eaten the cake without him."

"We would never do that," Aria proclaimed as she took Tessa's left hand.

Everly grabbed her right. "Well, it *is* chocolate, so I might think about taking a nibble, but I'd leave him some for sure," she murmured.

Tessa was laughing as the door swung wide, the joy of the moment filling her heart as she took her first step into the sanctuary.

Henry was waiting near the pulpit, the ends of his sandy hair just brushing the collar of his dark blue suit. He had a white rose on his lapel, and his eyes were a soft misty shade that she knew would always speak to her of home.

He stepped forward, smiling into her eyes as the twins placed her hands in his.

"You are stunning," he said.

"So are we," Everly added.

Tessa heard a rumble of laughter coming from the pews. If she looked, she knew that she'd see Wren and Jessica sitting beside Ernie in the front pew, several of Henry's coworkers nearby. Behind them there'd be a sea of faces—Kayla, the chief, people from the congregation and from the diner, neighbors and friends of Henry's who'd seemed happy to add Tessa into their circle.

Her focus was on Henry. A lock of hair had fallen across his forehead, and she brushed it away.

"You are everything I didn't dare believe in when I came to Provincetown," she whispered. "I love you."

He smiled. "I love you, too. You are everything I didn't know I was looking for, and I am so thankful that I found you."

Pastor Walker cleared his throat, his eyes sparkling with amusement. "I hate to interrupt, but I believe we have a wedding to attend to."

"Yeah. Let the man get on with things. I want this shindig over with," Ernie called out.

"Ernie!" Betty whispered loudly. "Enough!"

"What? I haven't been in a suit since 1967, and you chose me the itchiest one on this side of the Mississippi!"

"I'll be choosing you an itchy casket lining if you don't quiet down!" Betty hissed.

The guests laughed again, the warmth of their happiness washing over Tessa.

The windows glowed pink with fading sun, the old floors glistened with muted candlelight. And, Henry was beside her, strong and true and steady.

He smiled, and her heart soared, her soul

seeming to reach for his. This was where she belonged. In this place with this man. She knew it the same way she knew that the sun would set and rise again, that one season would change into another. That time would continue on and that they would continue with it.

Side by side.

For as long as God allowed.

\* \* \* \* \*

*If you enjoyed this story,
don't miss the previous books in
the FBI: Special Crimes Unit series
from Shirlee McCoy:*

Night Stalker
Gone
Dangerous Sanctuary

*And be sure to pick up these other exciting
books by Shirlee McCoy:*

Protective Instincts
Her Christmas Guardian
Exit Strategy
Deadly Christmas Secrets
Mystery Child
The Christmas Target
Mistaken Identity
Christmas On the Run

*Available now from
Love Inspired Suspense!*

*Find more great reads at
www.LoveInspired.com.*

Dear Reader,

It's been thirteen years since my first Love Inspired Suspense book was published. In the years since, many things have changed. My children have mostly grown. I've moved several times. I've said hello to new friends and goodbye to some old ones. I've learned a lot about what it means to be part of a family created not just by blood but by the bonds of friendship, faith and community. It is through those bonds that I have been taught the incredible value of compassion, empathy and kindness.

For Tessa Carlson, life has never been easy. She grew up in tough circumstances and found herself in worse ones. She fled something intolerable and created a life that she could be proud of. When she sees a little girl being kidnapped, she knows that intervening could cost her everything she's worked for, but she's not willing to turn her away. As the past she's fled stalks her, she learns the true meaning of love and the beauty of second chances.

I hope you enjoy *Lone Witness*, the fourth book in the FBI Special Crimes Unit series. I love hearing from readers. You can reach me at shirlee@shirleemccoy.com, or find me on Facebook, Twitter or Instagram.

Blessings,
*Shirlee McCoy*

# Get 4 FREE REWARDS!

## We'll send you 2 FREE Books plus 2 FREE Mystery Gifts.

**Love Inspired®** books feature contemporary inspirational romances with Christian characters facing the challenges of life and love.

**FREE** Value Over **$20**

---

**YES!** Please send me 2 FREE Love Inspired® Romance novels and my 2 FREE mystery gifts (gifts are worth about $10 retail). After receiving them, if I don't wish to receive any more books, I can return the shipping statement marked "cancel." If I don't cancel, I will receive 6 brand-new novels every month and be billed just $5.24 for the regular-print edition or $5.74 each for the larger-print edition in the U.S., or $5.74 each for the regular-print edition or $6.24 for the larger-print edition in Canada. That's a savings of at least 13% off the cover price. It's quite a bargain! Shipping and handling is just 50¢ per book in the U.S. and 75¢ per book in Canada.* I understand that accepting the 2 free books and gifts places me under no obligation to buy anything. I can always return a shipment and cancel at any time. The free books and gifts are mine to keep no matter what I decide.

Choose one:  ☐ **Love Inspired® Romance**
Regular-Print
(105/305 IDN GMY4)

☐ **Love Inspired® Romance**
Larger-Print
(122/322 IDN GMY4)

Name (please print)

Address                                                                                    Apt. #

City                                        State/Province                          Zip/Postal Code

### Mail to the **Reader Service:**
**IN U.S.A.:** P.O. Box 1341, Buffalo, NY 14240-8531
**IN CANADA:** P.O. Box 603, Fort Erie, Ontario L2A 5X3

**Want to try 2 free books from another series! Call 1-800-873-8635 or visit www.ReaderService.com.**

---

# Get 4 FREE REWARDS!

## We'll send you 2 FREE Books plus 2 FREE Mystery Gifts.

**Harlequin® Heartwarming™ Larger-Print** books feature traditional values of home, family, community and—most of all—love.

**FREE** Value Over **$20**

---

**YES!** Please send me 2 FREE Harlequin® Heartwarming™ Larger-Print novels and my 2 FREE mystery gifts (gifts worth about $10 retail). After receiving them, if I don't wish to receive any more books, I can return the shipping statement marked "cancel." If I don't cancel, I will receive 4 brand-new larger-print novels every month and be billed just $5.49 per book in the U.S. or $6.24 per book in Canada. That's a savings of at least 19% off the cover price. It's quite a bargain! Shipping and handling is just 50¢ per book in the U.S. and 75¢ per book in Canada.* I understand that accepting the 2 free books and gifts places me under no obligation to buy anything. I can always return a shipment and cancel at any time. The free books and gifts are mine to keep no matter what I decide.

161/361 IDN GMY3

Name (please print)

Address                                                                      Apt. #

City                                    State/Province                         Zip/Postal Code

**Mail to the Reader Service:**
**IN U.S.A.:** P.O. Box 1341, Buffalo, NY 14240-8531
**IN CANADA:** P.O. Box 603, Fort Erie, Ontario L2A 5X3

**Want to try 2 free books from another series? Call 1-800-873-8635 or visit www.ReaderService.com.**